Little Plum

Praise for
Little Plum

'I didn't so much read *Little Plum* as breathe it. Laura McPhee-Browne has an extraordinary ability to summon the ordinary and fill it with such significance and beauty that one has no choice but to inhabit her novels. At once exquisite and unsettling, dark and tender, *Little Plum* is a triumph.'
Hannah Kent

'Reading McPhee-Browne feels like listening to your own heartbeat.'
Amanda Lohrey

'An embodied and magical novel—so dark and earthy, colourful and frightening.'
Ellena Savage

'*Little Plum* draws us so lightly into the depths that we don't know how far it's taken us until we can't go back. With dark insight and masterly grace, Laura McPhee-Browne reminds us that our bodies can know things we don't, that experience can save or afflict us, and that possession can invest us with beautiful and terrible things.'
Ronnie Scott

'The pleasure of reading *Little Plum* comes from Coral's inner world...McPhee-Browne's writing feels honest and open.'
Books+Publishing

Praise for
Cherry Beach (2020)

'Captures beautifully the emotional state of early adulthood.'
Fiona Wright, *Sydney Review of Books*

'A vibrant, tender debut…I loved every minute of it.'
Laura Elizabeth Woollett

'Tender, bruising, sexy and heartbreaking in equal measure.'
Adelaide Review

'A beautiful, heartfelt book.'
Kill Your Darlings

'Gorgeously written.'
InDaily

'McPhee-Browne's exacting language
[is] evocatively decadent.'
Saturday Paper

'An exciting addition to this generation of writers.'
Overland

'[Presents] unadulterated queer womanhood…
Lusciously evocative.'
Meanjin

'A compelling examination of love and loss in all their guises.'
Australian Book Review

Laura McPhee-Browne is a writer and social worker living in Melbourne, on Wurundjeri land. Her short stories have been published widely in Australia. *Cherry Beach* (2020), her first novel, won a NSW Premier's Literary Award.

lauramcpheebrowne.com

Little Plum

Laura McPhee-Browne

TEXT PUBLISHING MELBOURNE AUSTRALIA

The Text Publishing Company acknowledges the Traditional Owners of the country on which we work, the Wurundjeri people of the Kulin Nation, and pays respect to their Elders past and present.

textpublishing.com.au

The Text Publishing Company
Wurundjeri Country, Level 6, Royal Bank Chambers, 287 Collins Street,
Melbourne Victoria 3000, Australia

Published by The Text Publishing Company, 2023

Book design by Imogen Stubbs
Cover photographs from Stocksy
Typeset in Bembo by J&M Typesetting

Printed and bound in Australia by Griffin Press, an accredited ISO/NZS 14001:2004 Environmental Management System printer

ISBN: 9781922790064 (paperback)
ISBN: 9781922791191 (ebook)

A catalogue record for this book is available from the National Library of Australia

The paper in this book is manufactured only from wood grown in sustainable regrowth forests

For all those who mother

Little plum,
said the mother to her son,
I want to bite,
I want to chew,
I will eat you up.

—ANNE SEXTON, 'HANSEL AND GRETEL'

They say, but where is your baby
And I say, no no, my baby my baby
They say, yes yes, look at your beautiful baby

—DOROTHEA LASKY, 'THE BIRTH'

I carried my fear of the world
to my children, but they refused it.

—MAGGIE SMITH, 'WHAT I CARRIED'

AMETHYST
The Stone of the Mind

Dream

I am at my mother's house, though it is also a mansion, and she is also a mother I never had but longed for, the kind who knows and sees. We are sitting on a couch I recognise, in a room I don't. She tells me something I have always wanted to hear, in a voice so quiet I have to ask her to repeat it. She says she won't, and becomes my whole mother, without the parts I wish for painted on. She stands and screams; I stand and scream back. She tells me she never wanted to be a mother; I tell her it hurts to hear that. I cry and rage, and she laughs at me. When I wake up, my fists are clenched so tight I have to punch the mattress to soften them.

1

THIS STORY IS about Coral.

Coral is twenty-nine years old, and she doesn't know what she wants. She has been doing an online dream course in her spare time, curated by Jungian analysts in America. The dream course suggests that she keep a dream diary, and because she wants the course to show her something, she writes down her dreams every morning, in a notebook lined with blue.

It has become apparent that she often dreams about her mother.

When Coral was a toddler, her mother let her eat anything she wanted: sand, sticks, playdough, puffs of dust from the corners of their tired old terrace house. Once, her mother tells her annually, they were at the park and Coral wandered off and came back to show her mother a ladybird she had placed on the tip of her little pink tongue, which she promptly swallowed. It makes Coral's mother laugh with delight to relay this, and confuses Coral. She believes ladybirds to be special, and can't imagine wanting to eat one—to vanish it into her tummy. She will never understand why her mother didn't try to get her to spit the poor beetle out. Sometimes she believes it has resurfaced and she can feel it in her throat—drowning, scrambling.

Coral's mother is petite, with a shrill voice and delicate ankles, and her name is Topaz. The gemstone topaz can be toxic, because it contains aluminium, though you wouldn't know it. Coral and Topaz have a gnarled relationship, and have grown together over the years in different directions. There is love there, between them, as well as pain and distortion. There is also a strange lightness, a kind of insouciance, in the way they communicate with each other most of the time. Coral prefers it this way. She also wonders whether Topaz is capable of anything else.

Coral and her mother are meeting to eat dinner together. It is Sunday, and it is late December—that week between Christmas and New Year's Eve. The city is sleeping off a long year, letting the heat hold it hostage.

They meet at Coral's local Italian, as they always do, and Topaz is late, as she always is. The shy waiter hands Coral the menu that is bigger than a newspaper, and moves backwards a few steps and then a few more, until she is behind the counter again. The waiter's body is alert, and Coral imagines that if she flicks her hand even just a small amount, the waiter will be back to take her drink order.

Coral would like a cold glass of white wine, but lately she

drinks wine quickly, and can't seem to slow down as each wave of muddled warmth laps at her. If she drinks slowly, the waves disappear, and it feels less bearable to be in the shallows these days. She wonders if she could drink a whole glass and order another to have just one sip before Topaz arrives, so it will appear that she has only had the one sip. She can feel the waiter watching her, and turns her eyes to smile and welcome a visit. She orders a glass of the house white and unclenches her thighs to enjoy it.

When the glass is almost empty, Topaz arrives, and comments on Coral's drinking and her hair and her blouse before Coral has had a chance to ground herself. Topaz is wearing a large ring with a blue stone, and tells Coral it is labradorite—for expanded spirituality. She asks Coral what she will order to eat.

'I think I'll have the gnocchi,' Coral answers. 'And another wine,' she adds.

Topaz eyes Coral's glass and Coral's face and then her glass again, and titters.

'Are you celebrating something?' she asks.

'No, Mum. I'm not.'

'Well. I'm going to have the burrata salad.'

Topaz's mother—Coral's grandmother—also bore the name of a toxic gemstone. Beryl and Topaz lived alone after Topaz's father died of asbestos poisoning, aged thirty, when Topaz was only one year old. They had lived like that, enmeshed, until Topaz met Coral's father and moved out. Coral suspects that this hushed relationship at close quarters cooked their toxicity, brewed it, helping it to stay potent and strong. Coral's name, chosen by her father, evokes the pinkish calcareous skeletons secreted by marine polyps and used in jewellery making. She thinks about this as they feast—one on potato and cream, the other on rubbery cheese and leaves.

After dinner, Coral and Topaz kiss each other's cheeks outside the restaurant. A man tries to pass them on the footpath and Coral moves to let him but Topaz doesn't. She can be remarkably indifferent to the needs of others.

'Call me during the week, will you,' Topaz says, and with a slight skip of her two short legs, she is gone.

Coral walks to her flat slowly, letting the rhythmic wind guide her along the footpath, touching the stems and the petals of the flowers she passes on the way. She won't have any more to drink when she gets home, even though she would love to take one bottle and then another to the couch to sink in that secret way that feels so delicious. She will fill herself up with something else instead, some chips and a bar of chocolate (white, marbled, gooey inside), and then she will climb into bed.

Topaz had talked and talked through dinner, and afterwards had suggested Coral get dessert and had eaten the majority of it, ending up with a smudge of chocolate mousse on her upper lip. Coral had tried to ask her how she was feeling—Beryl only died six months ago, and Topaz doesn't seem to have understood it yet, or perhaps she has understood it so well that it has become abstract. She had answered that she was fine, and before Coral could ask more had launched into a detailed description of the plot of a television show she had been watching. Coral had let the wine carry her up above the table, so she could stretch and yawn and close her eyes.

She loves her mother—she does, she does—but it is an exhausting kind of love.

2

A FEW WEEKS later, two men kill their father in a drunken fight on a quiet street of a nearby suburb at one o'clock in the morning. Coral and her colleague Roy have been assigned to attend and write a breaking-news article, which will be read because it is gory and tragic. She works with Roy at one of the largest community newspapers, where they try to stay current and cover big stories to justify their existence, to be read. Two journalists for one story, no matter how big, feels decadent—as if they are one of the city papers, which they decidedly are not. Coral is relieved that she won't have to go alone.

A father slain by his offspring: patricide. It is objectively shocking. Coral is sensitive to stories involving fathers. She doesn't know her own. She imagines (when she lets herself) that he is the gentle parts of her, the parts that wince at the more caustic of her mother's comments and actions. Then she remembers that he is gone, he is the one who left, and Topaz is still here.

Arriving at the crime scene early in the morning, Coral watches the fog disperse as it licks the edges of the road she parks on, and the brick-veneer semi-detached house she walks towards, wrapped up like a present with orange tape. There is already a scatter of uniform and plainclothes talking, writing in notepads, nodding and shaking their heads grimly. She is anxious—thoughts circle—and she taps one thigh and clenches her jaw to contain herself.

She's been the first reporter among law enforcement like this just enough not to have any idea what to expect or how to behave—it's different every time. Rather than the disdain she expected to encounter from the police, who she was sure would see her as a hyena tearing flesh from the slaughtered body of a lion, she has experienced polite acknowledgement, co-operation, even camaraderie. Once, at the scene of a grisly murder-suicide, she was told a series of case-sensitive details by a detective, who then asked her out for a beer. She's been smiled at, taken aside and given advice, snubbed. Then there are the times when she doesn't exist: the times when no one acknowledges her at all.

Before she can get a sense of the climate this morning, Roy's car coughs down the street and putters out behind hers, so she walks over to wait for him to find his tape recorder, his pen, and to say hello. Roy is a senior reporter, in his fifties, as far as Coral can tell. He is easy to be around, and seems to like her, listening to her even when she doesn't know what she is trying to say. He is a slow-moving, sleepy kind of person with messy grey hair and eyebrows. Kindness seeps out of his skin, along with nicotine and a meaty tang.

'Coral.'

'Roy.'

They smile at each other, and Coral notices a brown stain on Roy's white shirt. It is likely coffee. He drinks a lot of it, and has beige teeth as a result. He's also holding a large reusable cup, which he brings up to his mouth to drink from before giving her a wry smile.

It's a long time before they can get much of an idea from anyone about what has happened. The white suits need extra time in the house and on the path to the front door, where two big kitchen knives still lie. They are told by a young cop with braces that the knives are very sharp.

'Had one of those blocks that sharpen the blades when they're in there, I reckon,' he says, standing with them as if he's one of them or they're one of him, hands in his pockets, swaying back and forth from toes to heels to toes to heels. He makes Coral nervous, though it is important to note that most people do.

After an hour of hanging about, the journalists are given a little time. The big papers have arrived, and they ask their questions first, because the police recognise them, and they stand taller in the mud. The father died after one son stabbed him in the heart, and the other kicked him in the head once he was on the ground. Coral takes in the information carefully and tries to place it in the part of her brain that will not obsess. She often finds the details of her work overwhelming, and can spend hours ruminating, detailing, ticking the same small tragedies off in her mind over and over until she is exhausted and bereft. Writing the article helps, but when it is a serious crime, with more than one reporter chiming in, Coral can't always word the horror the way she wants to, and this seems to mean that it never leaves her.

'Was there a dispute?' Roy asks.

The police don't know much more, they say. The sons aren't talking, and their elderly mother has dementia. Coral is interested to know that two adult sons who killed their ageing father still lived with him. She wonders if there is a distinct reason why they didn't leave home, or whether they just started to become like mould or moss, and couldn't easily be removed.

To her left, a man approaches Coral with a boom mic in his hand.

'You with the papers?' he asks, as if they are in the middle of a conversation. It is almost offensive that he is speaking to her like this, against such a backdrop.

He has brown hair made of ringlets, and is grinning. She can smell something like sage, or toothpaste.

'Yes. Telly?'

He nods and shrugs his shoulders, as if to say he wishes he weren't, as if he doesn't care.

Coral has never spoken to the television crew at a scene. They always seem to have inside access, and a plan that involves swaggering past other media and smoking cigarettes by the door with cameras on their shoulders. This man isn't like that. He's slightly too tall for his trousers, and has one thumb hooked into a belt loop, like a lopsided cowboy. It's the only part of him that makes her think of country music. The rest is more oboist in a high-school orchestra, or anthropology student.

They stand opposite each other, not saying anything. His curls fall in front of his eyes and he moves them back in a way that causes Coral to realise she is attracted to him. Gently, he pushes the hair behind his ear and grins again. Coral can't help her mouth smiling back.

'Jasper!' someone calls out from around the corner of the house and the man startles slightly.

'That's me,' he says, and shrugs those shoulders again. 'See you around?'

She nods with a face she hopes has not grown pink.

He places the boom mic on the ground (something she is sure he is not supposed to do) and pulls a pen out of his pocket, holding out the other hand towards her, asking her to hold out hers. She does and he takes it, turns her hand over and uses the inky black pen to write JASPER and a mobile number. Presumptuous, she thinks. Presumption suits him. His fingers on the lifeline of her palm are perfectly warm.

Roy and Coral manage to get some information from the senior constable on duty. She tells them that the father had been terribly abusive, and that his children had been unable either to break away from him or, finally, to live in his grasp. The constable is philosophical and empathetic, and she seems to want the reporters to have the full story. She concludes that both men will likely be charged with manslaughter, for they have been intellectually and physically disabled by their father's reign. You see, she says, they were not capable of cold-blooded murder, and neither could they be blamed for committing it.

In her car before she leaves, Coral furiously notes down a

few more observations before they disappear—how the back windows of the house were sticky-taped up with newspaper; how the newspaper's date was seventeen years ago; how a sick, yellow-coated dog lay out the back on a long lead. How the air smelt like gas, because after killing their father the boys had tried to do themselves in, and had failed. She makes sure not to rub off any of Jasper's phone number as she uses her hand to write, and wonders if she will call him.

⟡

When Coral gets home, she drops her bag on the floor and spends some time sitting still and quiet on the couch, thinking about the bloody knives and Roy's coffee stain and Jasper's fingers and his hair, and whether she should call him, and when, and whether she will ever live in a house with a front path and shutters (whether she will ever murder someone). Then she takes off her shoes and stockings and skirt, and curls up in bed in her suit jacket.

It's night when she wakes up, after a heavy nap. She feels dirty and useless for having slept so long, and makes amends by stripping her bed and washing all of the linens, wiping down the walls of her bedroom, then kneeling beside her bed to pray to something above or below. She types up her part of the article on her laptop and sends it off, before dinner and sleep again.

3

CORAL SENDS JASPER a text three days after they meet. He replies less than a minute later, too enthusiastically, and Coral finds herself smiling with her cheeks each time she thinks about it, for the rest of the day and until they meet for a date at a dark wine bar near her flat. It is late summer but the air is fresh and crisp, and Jasper takes his woollen hat off after he sits down opposite her in the small wooden booth, and shakes out his hair. Coral tries not to look at the pile of curls for too long, moving her eyes to his face, which is beaming directly at her—a splendid moon. She can tell he is the kind of person who is unafraid of his own feelings: a colourful stone among the sedimentary and metamorphic rock. It makes her feel a little loose, like she has been holding herself tight for too long.

They talk about their families. Coral tells Jasper about her mother, and because he asks so many questions, she tells him about her father, and her suspicion that she will carry the loss of him with her until she dies. He tells her that he hopes she will never die, and then about his mother and his father and his younger brother and how they like each other, but don't necessarily understand each other, and that this has always felt tolerable. They order bright green olives in water, and glasses of yellow cheese wine followed by glasses of bloody, silty red, and then Jasper ducks out and brings them back a box of chicken-salt chips and they eat them slowly, plucking them out with their fingers. He says some funny things and some strange things, and Coral has to stop herself from giggling more than would be appropriate, though she suspects he wouldn't mind. She goes to the toilet, and while she sits on the cold plastic hole she taps her palm against the toilet wall five times, to make sure.

Out on the street—they agreed they should leave—it is cold like clouds. Coral makes sure she doesn't step on the footpath lines (cut into the concrete) and ruin everything.

They decide on her place, though she knows it has a funny smell (fish and plastic, from the blocked range hood and the cheap blinds she put up when she moved in). Coral's bedroom feels inadequate with tall Jasper sitting on the bed. He asks her if he can take his socks off (she notes that they are thick, sticky, red-mud-coloured, with holes at each big toe), and then he smiles at her in a way that flips everything over—the room is perfect, and so is she, and he is thinking these things right now, as he admires her from across the doona. His hands are beautiful: they look like the hands in an accomplished still-life drawing. When he touches her cheeks and jaw with his fingers, holds her head to him with his arm, she can smell the chicken salt.

She is smeared with him and him with her by the time they finish, and he pulls himself up, heaving and breathing deeply, like a porpoise. She doesn't usually like whiskers, and his are beaded with tiny sweat drops, but she wants to lick them, all along and up and down, to suck on each strand. It feels disgusting, like something deep inside her has cracked open and is oozing and she can't stop it. She pretends she hasn't changed, and lets him hold her face with his big hands again, both hands this time, as though she is a precious object worth millions of dollars. She likes it.

In the morning, they don't wake until both their alarms have sounded, over and over: have infiltrated their quiet dreams (quiet, because all the volume has come out during the waking hours) and the sun has started to burn so bright that the windows might melt. Jasper tells her things while she pulls on her undies and tries to find the less ugly of her dressing-gowns and smooths her hair across her face to make sure it is at least neat—he says:

'You're so beautiful.'

'Come here.'

'Can I help with—'

'I hope I get to see you again.'

She doesn't say much, doesn't need to. As she holds the front door open she smiles and feels as if it's the first real smile she has given someone in a long time. She says:

'I hope so too.'

⟡

At work later that day, Coral sees Jasper standing in the break room, and her heart jumps around as she walks towards him, but it's not him: it's just Simon, who has been interning for the sport section. In the toilet, she sees Jasper's friendly face pop up over the stall as she wipes the last of a wee from her urethra. But it's not him: it's just a trick of the light, or a toilet ghost. She makes herself a coffee after that second time (maybe she's tired), and decides not to tell anyone.

4

CORAL IS READING a book about a changeling. She tells Jasper about it on their second date but he doesn't seem to be listening. His ear is cocked, yet his eyes are sliding all over the room—they are sitting at the back of another bar—and she feels like she should just stop, mid-sentence, and that he should have warned her there was the potential to bore him. Prickles of anger rise up her neck (fire ants) and then he is back, and he takes her hands in his and kisses them. He asks her to tell him more, though she wonders if he also needs her to repeat what she has said so far because he didn't hear it. She tells him that variations of the changeling myth exist in many countries: Ireland, Poland, Japan, Scotland, Spain, Germany, Wales. That there are people who believe that this was the story told about babies and children with disabilities back then, because they didn't know why it had happened, or what it was and what to do. That there are people who believe there must be a fairyland, if so many societies believed in it.

He asks her some questions but doesn't wait to hear the answers and keeps kissing her lips when she is trying to speak. He seems to think this is funny and endearing, but it feels like he is suffocating her, like she could drop dead and he would tell the police he had only been joking.

'You're so sweet,' he says, though he has no proof of this.

Coral doesn't feel sweet. She feels savoury, like she's at risk of being opened up and salted and eaten against her will. As they talk, she feels more and more unsure of what she thought she and this man, Jasper, might have had on that first night, and she drinks every glass of wine he gives her and some she gives herself when she toddles to the bar. She can't say exactly why she does this (drinks like a fish) but she supposes she rather likes oblivion, and the drink seems to dissolve the negative thoughts. She wants to have sex with him again, for the physicality of it and so she can take off her clothes in front of him and watch his pupils dilate. She tries to slow down her sips so she will remember it in the morning.

They go to his place this time. He lives with others, and tells her about them, vaguely—three men his age, who are messy and loud but often at their girlfriends' houses. It's a fourth-floor flat in a large brandy-cream-coloured building she has seen many times but never really looked at, a five-minute drive from where she lives. He touches her all over in the taxi, tries to put a big rough hand between her legs, but she squeezes them shut. She doesn't need to feel good quite yet, and she won't share her vagina with him like a fruit platter, like an inside-out mango, a halved and pitted plum.

He tries to peel her like a banana (there are no further fruit analogies: she is determined not to be his crimped tomato or his melon ball) after unlocking his front door and almost, almost dragging her through but perhaps just guiding her. She removes his hands from her clothes, looks up at him and sees that his eyes are the colour of a stagnant pond she saw once in a dark garden. She imagines gnats or mosquitos floating around his face at night when he sleeps, deciding where to land.

'Not yet,' she says, with the throat of ten glasses of wine, and he hears her.

His room smells like sweat and is lit up by the huge moon in the window—Coral's familiar. Topaz often talks about how much Coral loved the moon when she was a little girl; how she would ask every night to go outside and look up at it, and for Topaz to tell her stories about who lived there, on its pale surface. She still loves to go outside and see it, but she doesn't do it much anymore—another joy that has dropped off in adulthood.

They lie down on his bed together and breathe on each other with their mouths because that's what happens when bodies lie close to each other and faces are adjacent. She wants him inside her again, to feel that tight sweet squeezy feeling that is sometimes like a bubble popping and sometimes like a sigh. She is on top first and it feels so good that she moves faster and faster, back and forth on him and against him, to keep the feeling going. He is glistening in the light of the moon and droplets slip off her skin onto his. She is hotter than she had realised: his room is a hot box, and maybe this is because he has plants growing in his cupboard or because they are both drunk and pulsating with a desire that doesn't make sense—the kind of desire that can create a hot box. It certainly can't create much else, once the quaking is over.

Afterwards, Coral pats herself dry with some toilet paper in the bathroom. They fall asleep quickly, side by side but as far apart as possible on his stinking bed.

5

THE HOT-BOX SEX (or the sex in the room that smells like fish) creates a foetus, and Coral first learns that this foetus exists after she vomits up her breakfast on the side of the road on her way to work one morning five weeks later and buys a pregnancy test on her lunchbreak. She wees on the stick in the work toilets and scrolls her phone while she waits, still dripping a little into the bowl below her. When she sees that two faint pink lines have appeared, her tummy gets up and tries to scamper, but there is the skin of the body that surrounds it and so it can't escape. She keeps sitting on the toilet until she thinks it will become a problem that she's not at her desk, then stands, wipes herself and straightens her skirt. She's pregnant, and it's Jasper's, and they haven't even texted since that night with the moon watching. She had hoped they would never see each other, would never text again.

There is a large jasmine bush outside the window her desk faces, and it prompts her to start thinking of names, as if she is fine with what she has just discovered, as if it is not a disaster. She thinks of purple names, like Violet, Lilac, Amethyst, Mauve. For a boy, Indigo or Periwinkle (Peri for short). If she keeps the baby, she will name it after a stone, she decides, twisting the ring set with an onyx on her middle finger.

The rest of the afternoon is spent editing a piece on aged-care standards that Coral has been writing for three days and isn't happy with. A weak nausea lingers, and she nibbles at the water crackers she stuffed in her desk drawer weeks ago, after an indecisive trip to the supermarket. She stuffed some basil dip in the work fridge on that day too, but the thought of it makes her tongue feel wet and oily.

⟡

It is tempting to deny the thing inside her and so she does, for the next week or so. The nausea comes each morning and sometimes in the afternoon, making her vomit up everything she eats, except salted pretzel sticks. She loses weight without even realising, until her jeans are a bit too big instead of a bit too small.

She has time to decide to abort this thing, Coral reminds herself each night. She can wander through the day ignoring her condition almost entirely, but at night it's different. Wherever she sits or lies—on the couch or the bed or the living-room floor, at the kitchen table slumped forward with her ear on her wrist at the pulse—her mind speaks at her urgently.

A problem shared is a problem halved, so she calls her friend Amber and asks if they can meet. She is about six weeks along, she thinks. Time to sort it out.

6

AMBER IS WAITING when Coral arrives at their favourite cafe on Saturday morning. Her nausea has momentarily lifted, and she has decided she can order something with vegetables, or meat, or eggs. She has known Amber forever, and they are so different that it grates sometimes, grates on each of them in different ways, and Coral wonders at these times how they can possibly be friends. Amber is lithe, with hair the colour of wet sand. She is always immaculately presented, slightly cold (her fingertips are icy) and sure of herself. They were little girls together at creche and then kindergarten and then primary school. Coral remembers she often walked slightly behind Amber, because Amber knew where she was going.

Amber orders the same thing every time: waffles covered in icing-sugar snow, without the vanilla ice-cream. She used to ask for the ice-cream to be served separately, in a little silver bowl, and would give it to Coral, who loves sweet things. Then one day she just asked for no ice-cream and Coral made sure to keep her face straight. She is reminded, as she approaches the table, that she used to wait for Amber to smile, that she would wonder whether Amber actually liked her or merely found her tolerable. Now she knows Amber rarely smiles at anyone, and that she loves Coral dearly.

'Hi, Amby,' Coral says, hanging her coat on the back of the chair and leaning down to brush cheeks. She has doggedly used nicknames for years, despite rolled eyes and pursed lips. It feels wrong to use the full name of someone she has known for so long.

'Hi,' Amber replies, her lips lifting upwards and her pupils dark against pale blue. There is a glass of black liquid beside her, likely chlorophyll and charcoal.

Coral sits, and asks Amber how she is. There's a tightness to Amber's forehead that isn't always there, a heaviness to her jaw.

Amber sighs and picks up her glass of darkness to take a long sip. 'It's not the best time, actually.' She wipes her mouth with a napkin, turning it grey.

Coral imagines reaching over and pulling the napkin from Amber's hand, putting it into her own mouth like it is a delicious piece of bread, chewing it up and swallowing as much of it as she can. She often has these sorts of thoughts when she is with Amber: as if a small part of her wonders what it would take to ruin everything. She should ask very carefully why it is not the best time for Amber, lest she lose the opportunity to be a sounding board, a comfort. She has done that before, witnessed Amber beginning to open, only to too eagerly involve herself and watch Amber close again, her pearl staying private in her oyster.

'Want to talk about it?' Coral finds her index and middle fingers locking together under the table without her permission, for luck. She wants to be close to her friend so much that her body pre-empts her. To pause after this question is difficult but it's what Amber would want, and Coral knows this.

They wait together at the table, Coral wondering when a waiter might come to see if she wants coffee. She would like a milky drink in a big mug, and hopes it will stay in her stomach. She would rather not wave someone down, though: it makes her feel like she thinks she is entitled to service. Amber is comfortable with waving—she asks for what she wants.

When Amber gets the attention of a bored young girl wearing a pair of Converse and a half-apron, she orders her waffles without the ice-cream, and her Earl Grey with a side of soy. Coral takes a deep breath and orders toast with eggs and bacon and beans and something to do with beetroot, and a large cappuccino. She crosses her toes to make sure her tummy holds out. After the girl sighs and turns on her sneakers to leave, Amber and Coral sit opposite each other, waiting.

Amber sighs, and moves her hair from one side of her long face to the other with a slender hand. Coral catches the glint of her engagement ring. Her fiancé, Micah, is a small and gentle man who Coral imagines to be so tender in bed that she would blush.

'My grandma's dying,' Amber says, her eyes becoming slightly swimmy. 'In Poland. Mum wants me to go over and meet her before she dies.'

Coral remembers that Amber has a living grandmother, and that her name is something like Gosha, Gosia, Gossa? Coral had liked the name when she heard it. She'd wondered at the time what it meant, and googled to find out that it meant pearl.

'Oh, no. Gosha?'

'Gosia.'

'Gosia! That's it. I'm so sorry.'

Amber looks at her directly, eyes suddenly dry. 'Thank you.'

'Will you go?' Coral asks. 'I guess you might not be able to?'

Amber's eyes are down now, and she clears her throat and folds her napkin squarely, placing it on the table before looking up at Coral again. It could be said that her movements are solemn, or weighted with grief, but Coral thinks she might know Amber better than that. She is just taking her time.

'I'd like to go, actually, so I'll try to get the time off work.' She picks up her glass of water and takes a long drink. 'I'd rather not go on my own, though.'

Coral nods, and imagines Amber in Poland on her own. Having never been to Poland, she can't imagine the whole scene, but can clearly see Amber frustrated and lost in her own contained way. Amber doesn't speak Polish and she doesn't enjoy new places unless she has chosen to be there. Coral sees small beads of sweat swelling on Amber's upper lip in her imagination, and this never happens to Amber in real life.

'Do you want to come with me?'

The question is so unexpected that Coral is nodding after she hears it, out of habit, and has to stop herself. 'Me?'

Amber smiles with the corners of her eyes.

'Yes, you.'

'Wow,' Coral replies.

'It would have to be very soon. Could you?' Amber is businesslike again.

'Yes!'

Coral will work out how she can go to Poland later (she feels a quiver in her belly that could be the beginnings of the baby or excitement). If she has to take leave without pay, she can use her savings. She'll tell Amber about the pregnancy next time. Or maybe on the plane.

Coral sees two plates coming towards them. She taps the underside of the table for luck, for luck that she can eat the food, and for luck that she can keep living, that she won't do something wrong.

They finish their breakfasts quickly. Amber has a dentist's appointment, but Coral is suddenly ravenous, demonstrative. She tries to get a waiter's attention to ask for more beans, but no one sees her.

7

IF CORAL COULD, she would have a drink. Coral *could* have a drink, because one glass of alcohol is an acceptable amount for pregnant women to drink these days, at least according to most people she knows. If Coral could have just one drink, she would. But she would rather have many. She imagines the glitter of a glass of sparkling wine in front of her, on her desk: its ability to change how she is feeling into something more like water than land.

Her manager, Steve, was as displeased as she'd expected when she arrived that morning and asked to speak with him, requesting almost immediate leave. Her lie about needing the leave because her mother was sick led to Coral calling Topaz twice to see how she was. Topaz was cheerful and slightly chiding, as always, which helped salt any guilt from Coral's heart.

Despite Steve's displeasure—his grunts and sighs and vague threats—the leave is approved. Coral hasn't taken any time off since she started as a cadet, thirteen months ago. When she imagines spending two weeks without an alarm waking her in the morning, without the wait for the tram that is always early or late, without coffee made from a plastic pod, she can feel the freedom at her heels. She can't imagine Poland yet, or two weeks with Amber in airports and hotel rooms—they haven't spent time like that together since they were kids. Amber will be difficult to read in an airport and on an aeroplane. Her natural way of communicating is suited to the passive chaos of transit, because she doesn't mind directly asking for exactly what she needs—the waiting time, another glass of water, better seats. She will go into action mode, and Coral will be left behind.

She spends the rest of the day thinking about what would happen if she asked her friend Ruby to meet her at the pub after work and they got really quite drunk together, if she just pretended that she didn't know she was pregnant. She imagines it would be mostly a relief, and a little bit horrific. Or perhaps the other way around, since she might be starting to move towards a beholding for the thing inside her. Ruby loves to drink, and so does Coral, and they often spend the night together at a beer-garden table buying jug after jug of the cheapest beer on tap—becoming so sentimental and amorous that in the morning it feels like she has been spat out, sticky and alone. She won't text Ruby, because if they do meet up and she doesn't drink, to save the baby, Ruby will wonder why, and she isn't ready to tell anyone. She can share anything with

Ruby, really, without worrying that Ruby will judge her, or have such a steadfast opinion that Coral will immediately feel at sea. Despite this, something is stopping her from sharing the news, and she doesn't want to ignore it.

⟡

The work day rolls out slowly. The piece she is writing with two other cadets about a mysterious pest that is killing fruit trees (plum, apricot, peach) in the Yarra Valley feels irrelevant. Sometimes when she is writing at work she starts to think about who will actually read these words she is trying to put in the right order. She pictures people skimming over the articles she has worked on, their interest never piqued, until the word 'worthless' echoes against her skull. It helps to shake her head when these thoughts come, to rustle them up, to shush them.

She calls one of the fruit growers who has dealt with hundreds of her trees rotting and dripping and oozing until they died. This grower is trying to get support from the state government to find out what killed them.

'No one will listen to me,' she hears the woman say, far off in a farm kitchen, warm and sad. 'Whatever's doing this has never been here before. It's ferocious. And it's not leaving.'

Coral tells the woman she is sorry more than is helpful and rings off, feeling as if she needs to do something. It sounds like the trees have been eaten alive by a horde of tiny, gnashing beasts, and the woman like she has been broken by the experience of watching them die and the lack of support she has received. Coral knows very little about trees or stone fruit or orchards or climate or critters, but she hopes she can write something that will convey the grief and loss this woman is experiencing, and that it might spur other growers to come forward.

Despite wanting to be a journalist, Coral does not enjoy trying to get people to talk to her, though she is often glad she has done the work once a conversation has happened. It can be overwhelming to ask people questions and take on the responsibility of using their truth in a way that is productive. Coral doubts her work over and over, but she has learned not to let it bring her all the way down.

She sees Roy in the staff kitchen in the afternoon, both of them searching for a biscuit. He looks so tired she wants to tell him to lean against her so he can have a brief rest. Instead, she scrambles through every cupboard until she locates a fresh packet of Classic Assorted, encourages him to take all six of the Scotch Fingers before taking two Custard Creams for herself, and asks him how his day has been.

He sighs, pushes a finger of biscuit into his pink mouth. 'It's been grim. You?'

'Yeah, pretty grim,' Coral says, though today isn't any more or less terrible than any other day, and it has a sheen over it. She wonders whether the sheen has been provided by the moon, and decides to google where they are in the lunar cycle when she gets back to her desk.

They can't say much more about the grimness in the staff kitchen, so they mumble farewells and leave. She likes Roy, and appreciates how melancholy he can be. It feels like his presence could split open something fake, and that is nothing short of powerful.

By five she has finished a draft, and she emails it to Steve for feedback. It is pleasing to have written something, for writing is nothing if not proof of existence, and Coral wants to exist. She imagines what he will type in reply: 'Expand!' or 'What does this mean?'

It is time to leave the office and head out onto the street, to walk a few blocks and wait for a tram to take her home. She can see late-afternoon sun on the jasmine outside her window, and it triggers a warmth in her blood that reminds her of a glass of golden box wine. She won't text Ruby, though she wants to see her. She doesn't have anything to say, and if they did meet up she would just wish she was drunk so she could speak silly things and not care so much, so she could stop her chanting thoughts from interfering.

On the tram home a man sits down opposite her and opens up a kebab, eating it with such abandon that he gets garlic sauce all over his chin. The smell of the meat renders her, all of a sudden, violently nauseated. She vomits in a bin after alighting at her stop, and wipes her trembling mouth with one clean sleeve.

8

CORAL FEELS SICK all that week, every morning and all through every afternoon. Sometimes the night is worse than the day, and she can't bear to eat anything except the occasional cracker or sheath of lettuce. She vomits sometimes, but nothing really comes up, except gelatinous stomach water. Coral cries as she vomits because it hurts her torso and throat. She doesn't cry because she is going to be a mother. She thinks she might be excited about that part.

After a week the sickness becomes almost normal, though it affects her mood substantially. She gets used to the saliva waiting inside her mouth before she vomits, but not the dread. She thinks of the pregnant women who end up in hospital because they are so sick they need to stay on a drip, and she is horrified for them. Her stomach has butterflies in it every day too, more than it usually does, and they are flapping harder than they usually would. Sometimes she feels like she can't breathe, just for a few seconds, because the butterflies have travelled up to her chest. She should go to see her doctor, to get confirmation that something is growing in there, and to ask whether she can stay on her medication. She books an appointment online, her butterflies preventing her from calling the clinic on her mobile, and tries to take diaphragm breaths at her desk.

⟡

Coral meets Topaz for their Sunday dinner and wonders again what Topaz will say when she tells her she is pregnant. Coral always expects unhelpful responses from her mother, and is vindicated more often than not. She knows Topaz will have to confirm whether she is single: 'I thought you were, but perhaps you are not?' Despite her penchant for liberalism, Topaz seems to despise those who break certain societal rules, and is proud to be someone who has never come completely undone. Coral won't tell Topaz until she has to, until her belly is too big to hide. She wonders if her mother will react cruelly or be devastated.

They meet on the street outside the restaurant, arriving from opposite directions at the same time—for once, Coral is also a little late. Topaz waves her hand as she moves towards her daughter. Coral smiles as much as she can. Her mother is wearing a long purple dress, and when Coral says it is nice, Topaz tells her it would be nicer on someone tall, and that Topaz and Coral shouldn't wear floor-length dresses at their height. Coral doesn't ask Topaz why she is, in fact, wearing a full-length dress, and instead says, 'Oh, well.' She is tired, bone-tired. It's taking over from the nausea and the fear in a way that feels just as difficult. She orders sparkling water from the same shy waitress, hoping the fizz will give her some energy.

'And how is Amber?' Topaz asks. She always asks after Amber, though not after any of Coral's other friends.

Coral tells Topaz that Amber's grandmother in Poland is very sick and that soon they will fly over together to see her. She wonders whether it will remind Topaz of the recent loss of Beryl, but it doesn't seem to. Because it is Amber she has made this absurd plan with, Topaz doesn't bite, and instead seems to approve. Topaz and Amber's mother, Cecylia, were friends when Amber and Coral attended primary school together, though Cecylia has dropped off since then, preferring to mix with a crowd of rich women who run small businesses. Coral's heart scrunches when she remembers how hurt Topaz was by Cecylia's distance. Despite the rejection, Topaz remains fiercely loyal to Amber.

'Poland,' Topaz states, as if this says everything, and bites down on a piece of focaccia speckled with rosemary and salt.

'Yes,' Coral replies. 'Poland.'

Topaz's small teeth gnaw at the focaccia; there is a flake of pink salt on her upper lip. Coral's head wants to lean against the white fabric that covers their table, just to rest a short while. She has ordered a chicken-sauce pasta, and more focaccia, and hopes her stomach will let her eat it. She doesn't even feel like a glass of wine. Topaz has ordered an entree, veal carpaccio, and a glass of prosecco. When the glass arrives—gingerly placed in front of Topaz by the waitress—the bubbles seem particularly feisty. They are jumping out of the glass and popping in the cool air, the pale yellow of the liquid reflected in the early evening sun and lending Topaz's face a softening, a warming.

'I hope you'll be safe over there,' Topaz says, her eyes trying to catch Coral's across the table.

She isn't using the tone she has sometimes, the one that makes Coral uncomfortable, because it assumes too much: too much wisdom, or something. She sounds as if she is just saying that she cares.

Coral wishes she had more energy to show Topaz that she appreciates this. She responds carefully. 'I will, Mum. I promise. Amber's very sensible—you know that.'

Topaz nods quickly. Amber is very sensible. Not like Coral, who is having a baby with no one, with a man she has met twice and who might be awful. Not like Coral, who has a problem with alcohol and her thoughts and her nerves, and maybe they are the same thing and who knows which one came first, really; but she was never like Amber, not even in Prep, when they held hands in class because she had wet her pants and Amber noticed and knew she needed help. Not Coral, who might be just like her father, whose legacy is that he couldn't cope and ran away.

'Will you see the Baltic?' Topaz spits out a wet crumb of focaccia on the end of Baltic, and it lands in her prosecco. What a sad thing, to watch the small particle of bread bumble about in the glass, mussing up the clear liquid with the tiny bubbles that react to it, ruining the dazzling light show.

Coral doesn't know if she will see the Baltic. She hasn't even looked at a map yet, to see where it is in Poland they will be visiting. She has had to use every bit of her curiosity lately for work. When she finishes each day, she doesn't care to find out anything else about anything.

'I don't know.'

Topaz makes a small noise, somewhere between a scoff and a squeak. Coral suspects she is trying not to react with outright derision, and knows how hard this must be. She can give her mother a leg-up. She's so tired there's no energy for defensiveness, anyway.

'I don't really know where we're going! I should look into that, shouldn't I?' She laughs and gives Topaz a sheepish smile.

Topaz smiles back and pops the last of the focaccia in her mouth, poking her little tongue out to clean away the salt grains and flecks of rosemary. Happily, they sit for a second, Topaz no longer needing to tell Coral she is hopeless, Coral no longer needing to react.

The waitress arrives with their dishes, and she seems lighter, more willing to place the plates where she thinks they should go, rather than waiting to be directed. Coral has experienced this before—the way a conversation between two people can affect the energy of an entire space, an entire day, and all the people within it. When Topaz and Coral let some steam out of the bag, it seems that others follow.

They eat, and enjoy each other's company as much as they can, before Topaz insists on paying for everything and they agree to talk during the week on the phone before they meet again, next Sunday. Outside, on the nature strip, Topaz wraps a pashmina around herself like a blanket, and kisses Coral's cheek. Coral smells her mother's face powder, and her perfume, and her Russian Red lips.

'Have a look at a map, will you?' Topaz asks, patting Coral's shoulder. 'It's good to know where one is going.'

Coral's walk home is sober and slow. She places her hands on her stomach a few times as she moves through the backstreets of Carlton. It doesn't feel any bigger, but then perhaps it does. Did she always have that rounded part, or is that where the baby is growing, where it is pushing her skin forwards to carve out a tiny room of its own? She stops and googles '7 weeks pregnant' on her phone. The baby is the size of a small blueberry, with little nubs for arms.

She hopes it's a girl. She can't imagine having a baby boy. This sudden thought makes her feel like she must step over every crack she comes across, in order to avoid the thought becoming a reality. It's tiring to step over all of them, and when she gets to her door she is puffing. She lives alone, so there is no one inside to wonder why she is so flushed. In order to live alone, she has to rent a place so small that it clings to her. Tonight will be a particularly clingy night: she can feel it in her fingers and her toes.

9

CORAL ASKS TO have Tuesday morning off work, to see her doctor. Steve is appalled by her request, but she doesn't really care. The other cadets talk about how furious he always is, and this helps Coral to ignore the heat from the furnace. If he is angry all the time at everyone, it doesn't have to feel personal, though she wishes he would calm down. She has never been good at not worrying, not taking things so personally that people's reactions don't feel like slaps to her face with their shaking hands, but since she has been pregnant there hasn't been much energy for anything but the pregnancy itself. It feels surprisingly right to focus entirely on the little piece of fruit in her womb.

Dr Shelley Carver is an older woman with a mass of red fuzzy curls that she wears in a bushel around her face, which is always made up in cream and powder. Coral has seen Dr

Carver since she was a little girl, when Topaz would take her for her immunisations and to check her weight and height and head circumference. She saw Dr Carver when she first got her periods and they were painful and irregular, and when she realised that the obsessive thoughts she was having were disintegrating her from the inside out. She loves Dr Carver, who seems to think how Coral feels is important, noteworthy. It always seems to be a bright day when she visits her consulting rooms on a leafy street in Carlton North. Every time Coral leaves the clinic, she takes a moment to sun herself.

The terrace house Coral grew up in is only a few streets away from the surgery. She and Topaz shared a rental with two other adults—Lou and Irene, friends of her mother's who also couldn't afford to sprawl out on their own—until Coral was eighteen. Two grown adults who were not related to her witnessed her growing up, which she can't see as anything but intimacy, and she still doesn't understand how they did it. She would have cried as a baby and been under their feet as a toddler, and yet all she remembers from Lou and Irene is a detached kindness.

Topaz and Coral had the second of the three storeys to themselves: two cramped bedrooms and a balcony, with their very own plastic toilet. The adults did their own thing most of the time, but there was dinner together in the kitchen some nights, television together in the high-ceilinged lounge, and Coral remains grateful that these two people shared many of their precious years with her, while she grew. Despite this, she has no nostalgia for the house. It was damp and dark most of the time, and she wasn't ever necessarily very happy there.

When she moved out after finishing school, into a share house out west in Footscray, she realised she hadn't really ever been able to breathe.

Coral waits on one of the upholstered chairs in reception, too tired to flick through magazines from the early nineties that sit, shiny and dated, on a table in the room's centre. The magazine on top is a gardening one, or about houses and homes. The image on its cover is a basket full of plums, nestled together, the colours of bruises. There are other people waiting, too, and they are all on their phones. Dr Carver does not run as late as some doctors, though she doesn't quite keep to schedule. This, Coral assumes, is because she tries to give each patient the time they need.

Coral can wait today. She doesn't want to be in the office, and her mouth and stomach are at the edge of nausea. The older woman perched two seats from her is eating small pieces of something that she carefully takes out of her handbag and places quietly in her mouth. She moves her hand in and out of the bag so skilfully, it is impossible to work out what she is eating. Coral assumes nuts or seeds, or small bits of torn-off bread from an oblong roll. She can't smell anything: something to be thankful for. Smells have hounded her these past few weeks, almost none of them pleasant or friendly. It seems inappropriate for this woman to be furtively eating in a doctor's surgery, though perhaps it is fine or common, or both. Coral won't ask her to stop—it takes a lot for Coral to ask someone else to stop what they have decided it is perfectly acceptable to do. She remembers only one time that she broke through her own doubt and asked a man near a lake to stop throwing stones at the ducks. He had laughed and thrown his next stone at her, and she had fled.

The tapping has increased, and so have the circling thoughts, and they are not cancelling each other out like they sometimes do. She needs to tell Dr Carver this.

She used to tap things in order to tackle a new idea, or something she had been asked to do, or when her brain got caught in a thought loop and she had to break it free. In primary school she would be asked to stop tapping the desk before she had even realised she was doing it, often before a test or when she was picked to answer a question. Some of her teachers had been kind about it, asking to speak to her after class and gently wondering if she was feeling worried about anything, if the tapping helped calm things down. Others had been frustrated, unable to tolerate it, and she tapped more in those classes, as if her body was more rebellious than her brain.

She was on medication for obsessive-compulsive disorder before she got to high school. The tablets helped, as did talking to the psychologist Topaz paid for every week, who seemed to understand exactly why her body needed to make sure of the objects around it and how she could begin to trust more. She kept seeing the psychologist for years, until she believed she was so stable that she no longer needed to. The medication she still takes; it makes her calmer, and sometimes opaque.

'Coral?'

Her name is called from behind her, and she turns to see Dr Carver's face and Dr Carver's body, draped in lustrous fabric, standing at the doorway of the hall that is a spine for the consulting rooms. Coral has been called before anyone else she has been waiting with, which seems lucky. She hefts herself up (it already feels like she is carrying something, though the thing itself is nothing more than a berry) and smiles at Dr Carver, who turns and leads her down the corridor.

'How are you, Coral?' Dr Carver faces her in the light-filled room lined with framed photos—the doctor with her partner, Ian, and their three huge husky dogs—and credentials.

'I'm pregnant,' Coral replies. She had planned not to say this at once, but is unable to stop herself from getting straight to the point, to the thing that she has been carrying around with her for weeks, on her own. Seeing Dr Carver again is like seeing someone you love when you are feeling sad and immediately bursting into tears. She can feel those tears pushing at the back of her eyes now, and she realises it is the emotion of it too that has been tiring her out.

Dr Carver doesn't say anything for a second, and keeps looking at Coral, her head bobbing ever so slightly. She usually takes her time responding, as if she is making sure to give space for further reflections, but this time it seems she might be speechless. Coral picks at one of her fingernails, then taps a hand against the leg of her chair.

'Well!' Dr Carver says, then, 'Well, I never!' in her best voice—the one that communicates through its tone that everything is fine, will be okay, is perfectly endurable.

'Shall we confirm that together now?' she asks, smiling at Coral, and Coral nods.

Dr Carver stands and picks through the piles of plastic and metal medical bits that cover the shelves and sink on one side of the office.

Coral realises that her body is clenched and she is breathing from her chest, and tries to release some of the holding by slowly filling up her diaphragm with air. She can hear Dr Carver muttering to herself: *Now, where did I put those—I was sure I ordered more of them.*

Then Dr Carver is back in her seat with gloves on, and she hands Coral a plastic jar with a sticker on it. 'Go and do a wee into that, then we'll take some blood to make sure.'

In the bathroom Coral locks the door and unbuttons her jeans, button by button. She drank two tall glasses of water from the tap before she left her flat that morning, assuming she would be asked to fill a cup. She is determined not to get any on her fingers—it's time she learned how her stream behaves—but she does, and has to wash her hands six times in the sink in order to convince herself she won't smell of urine. And would that be the end of the world, she asks herself, if you smelt like wee? What would happen? She still challenges herself when her thoughts start to tornado, though this rarely helps. How can you rationalise the irrational, her psychologist used to ask her. He would answer before she could every time: *You can't, so you don't.*

Back in Dr Carver's room she watches a stick get placed in her yellow liquid and set aside, and then it is just her and Dr Carver opposite each other, waiting for the stick to confirm or deny. It occurs to Coral all of a sudden that she might not actually be pregnant after all, and she considers what it will feel like if she isn't, if the test she took those few weeks ago in the staff toilets wasn't accurate. Devastating, she realises. She has so integrated this pregnancy into her life, her thoughts, that it would feel like a part of her had been removed, though it had never really been there. She pulls herself out of this contemplation and back to Dr Carver, who is watching her, a faint smile across her face, her hands placed neatly in her lap.

Coral needs to spit it out. 'If I am pregnant, can I stay on my medication?'

Dr Carver's hands stay where they are, one on top of the other. She nods. 'I expect so, yes. We know how much it helps you, and a pregnancy full of fear wouldn't be good for you or the baby.'

Coral can feel relief dripping through her but it doesn't wet her stomach. She can hear that she doesn't have to stop using the tool that helps, but if she could, she would—if she could, she should. She hears that staying on her medication while she is pregnant is not ideal, but that she will have to because she is sick, and she needs it, and that it is likely her sickness will be passed on to her child. To not have a chance to do things differently is such a familiar place to be that she shrugs, pushing the feelings away before they touch her.

'Could it hurt the baby?' she asks quietly.

'The medication could possibly hurt the baby, yes. But the baby would be more hurt if its mum had to suffer through nine months of acute stress.'

How will this possibly be all right? Coral wonders, and then Dr Carver pats her knee and gets up to check on the stick.

The test is positive, so Dr Carver sticks a needle into the soft inside of Coral's arm where the blue veins draw their wobbly lines. It stings, and it takes longer than she remembers it having taken when her blood has been needed before, but she always feels like that about everything. Her past is always rose-coloured, her present an inadequate puce.

Dr Carver recommends Coral sit a while after the needle has been pulled out and a tuft of cottonwool has been pressed against the wound, and gives her a handful of jelly beans to eat. There are two pink ones, one yellow, one almost black. She knows the black one should be liquorice and puts it in her mouth first, for the anise to spice her gums.

She will find out the test results in a few days, Dr Carver tells her, while the peppery lolly occupies her mouth. They agree that Coral will book an appointment for a week's time, to discuss things.

10

ON FRIDAY, CORAL gets a call from Dr Carver's clinic to tell her that her blood test has come back positive, that she is indeed pregnant. She works all day with a small smile on her face, then can't sleep all night because her throat is full of terror. Saturday is nausea—white and thick and cold, and then orange and hot and low in her thighs, almost. She has never felt so utterly wretched. On Sunday, she wakes up with only the chalk outline of that sick in her body, and texts her friend Ruby, suggesting they have a drink at the Marquis of Lorne that afternoon.

It's a hot early-autumn day, and they meet on the rooftop where the sun can shine directly down on their heads, warming their hairlines. Ruby is there when Coral arrives, looking at her phone, a glass of beer beside her. They hug and kiss each other's cheeks. Ruby smells like Palo Santo smoke and baby powder. She is sunkissed, her brown hair strewn with gold.

Coral puts down her lemon, lime and bitters—a drink she has never ordered before—and sees Ruby's eyes flick from the glass back to her.

'I'm not drinking at the moment,' she says, watching Ruby's beautiful broad face for movement.

'Yeah, I wondered, hey! Usually we don't meet on Sundays because you have dinner with your mum, and you don't want to be shit-faced?'

She could just agree and move on, but she has planned to tell Ruby and she wants to. She feels safe in Ruby's response, whatever it will be. There are other responses she is scared of, and a safe one first will help.

'Yeah, usually. But this time I'm not drinking because I'm pregnant.' She smiles, to show it is not necessarily a complete disaster.

Ruby doesn't move or make a noise for a second, then brings her hands to her mouth and squeals into them, loudly. People on the tables around them turn to look.

'Pregnant? You're pregnant?'

Coral nods, still smiling. Her hands have moved to her belly, where they cup the small something beneath her skin that is definitely there.

'Oh, Coral! Are you okay? That's so special—wow. Are you all right?'

Ruby cares about Coral, and Coral can feel the concern in her voice, a concern that can be alleviated because she trusts Coral and doesn't look down on her. It has always been like this between them, since they met in a pottery class when they were both twenty, trying to find something to do, outside of uni and drinking. Ruby had praised Coral's dimple mug, and made several of her own crouched vases.

'Yes, I'm okay!' And she is. 'I'm kind of excited.'

Ruby brings her in for a long, muffled hug, and a bit of her hair strays into Coral's mouth. It tastes like sweet herbs, like mint or basil, and Coral is suddenly ravenous.

'I might order some chips,' she says, and moves to stand. Without the headiness of a first beer, she is anxious. She doesn't know what to say—even to this friend she knows so well, who won't judge her. Ruby pulls at her to keep her sitting.

'Wait, babe! I'll order us some chips in a minute. I want to ask you things.'

Coral acquiesces, lets her body move into the moment, where she can be because she has only had something soft to drink. She will tell Ruby everything she is feeling, and how this happened. She knows it is good for her to speak.

'Is it that guy you met at the crime scene?' Ruby asks, with a gentle look on her face: soft eyes, two-pillow cheeks. 'Is it his?'

Coral nods.

'Does he know?'

'Nope.'

Ruby seems to accept this, as the sun beats down, and moisture begins to gather at Coral's cleavage and neck. She nods when Coral says she wants to keep the baby, and when Coral says she doesn't know why, or if it's the right decision. Coral tells her that she doesn't really like Jasper, that she wonders if he is a bit dodgy or weird, but that she knows she might wonder if men are strange more often than they actually are, because of her anxiety and all the possible equations.

'You have a good tummy for these things,' Ruby says, and places her hand on Coral's stomach, where the little thing is growing.

They both smile. It feels nice to have someone else's hand touch the part of Coral that she has been so obsessed with lately. Touching oneself seems to only go so far. She pictures Ruby's hand on her stomach in seven months, when there will be more to grasp.

'Jasper sounds like a bit of an idiot, but you can do this on your own, for sure. Or, not on your own, but with me and your mum, and Amber and Micah. And—'

Ruby doesn't finish this sentence, because there's not much else to say. She brings her warm cheek to Coral's and nuzzles it slightly, pulls her in for another hug.

'This will be a lot, though. You know that, don't you?' Ruby asks, her brow squeezed.

'Yes, Rubes, I know.'

The sky spins slightly above them, clouds moving fast like they do sometimes, as if in a hurry.

'Thank you,' Coral adds.

Ruby claps her hands and lifts her pint glass to take a long gulp. 'We will help you. It will be lovely!'

They sit and talk, about other things, then about the baby again, and Jasper and Poland and Amber. Ruby tells Coral she is lonely sometimes, without a partner, and Coral says that she is too. She doesn't tell Ruby that the baby seems already to have helped with her loneliness—like a small hand holding hers each day. It would be too much to admit that, when the baby is not much more than a blueberry, and could disappear or be aborted for many more weeks yet.

Coral texts Topaz and asks if they can reschedule their dinner, and Topaz replies immediately with a yes. Another unpredictable response from her mother, who Coral had assumed would ask questions.

The sunset in Fitzroy, where they see it a few hours later, happens as it often does in the heat: with a half-hearted cling that only drops once you are home and in the dark. The air as Coral walks towards her flat is smoky grey, potent with trodden hydrangeas. She had two lemon, lime and bitters, one orange juice, and a pint of soda water with a slice of lemon floating in it while Ruby drank her beers, and it wasn't as hard as it could have been. She missed the feeling of having a break from her own mind, her own body: the feeling of a lack of feeling that alcohol can bring. But her body has been different these past few weeks, and for once she doesn't want to hide from it.

That night Coral has many small dreams, all unfinished, all confusing. She wakes to take a sip of water from the glass next to her bed throughout: the dreams seem to be dehydrating her. Jasper is kissing her in one of them, and his tongue is so long and pointy that she realises he is actually a snake, and wonders how she had missed this. In the morning she updates her dream diary, and vomits chips and gravy into the toilet.

Dream

A small dream where I know my mother has died and I spit into a sink, look at my face in a mirror. I wake from this one crying. I quickly fall back to sleep.

A longer dream, if dreams can be small or long. I am sitting in a field of tall grass. It almost hides the horizon. The grass is yellow and the sun is bright above me. I am very comfortable, but I know my mother is coming, and when she arrives we hit each other across the face, the pain like shattering glass. Before I kill her, my heart and her heart in my hands, I wake.

1

THREE WEEKS LATER, Amber and Coral land in Poland. Coral is eleven weeks pregnant now, and the foetus is the size of a fig. The foetus was a raspberry, then a cherry, then a cumquat, and now it is a flushed and seedy fig, so sweet she can taste it. It is early April when they leave Melbourne and early April when they arrive, finally, in Warsaw, but the season is the opposite—they left behind autumn, still warm from summer, and walk out of the airport's sliding doors into early spring, decorated with the detritus of a Northern Hemisphere winter.

Amber has been good company so far. She can sleep on planes—unlike Coral, who can't get her body to relax enough—and she slept through most of their flights from Melbourne to Singapore, Singapore to Helsinki. Neither of them could afford a more straightforward journey, so they were stuck at Helsinki Airport for nine hours, walking through the clean, wide hallways until they found a Moomin-themed coffee shop, where they ordered blueberry milkshakes and Coral sent a silent prayer to Tove Jansson.

Coral noticed that everyone in the airport and on the plane from Finland to Poland was polite and quiet and well behaved, and she wondered if this was typically Finnish. The language that she picked up in snippets from those around her and from announcements, on the other hand, sounded like a complicated cross between Italian and German—two loud languages—and was unwieldy to Coral's ears. She couldn't quite marry these people and their tongue, realising late that she didn't have to.

The plane to Warsaw was small, and she and Amber were not sitting together. Next to Coral was a large, meek man with white-blond hair and thighs as thick as fir trees. He was so self-contained that he didn't crowd her, despite his size. She needed to use the bathroom often, and wished she had thought to book an aisle seat. It wasn't hard to ask the large man if he could let her out, but she would rather not have bothered him. He nodded his silky head and stood to let her through, again and again.

Coral is exhausted. The weeks since those hours spent with Ruby on a rooftop in Fitzroy have been a mad dash to try to ready herself for a journey across the world. There hasn't been time to consider that she is pregnant, or what she will do in six or so months when she has a newborn baby. Yet her sleep has been disrupted by a brain that won't quite stop trying to reason with itself, with the obsessive questions that flood it when the sky is dark, and a body that feels itchy on the inside. She is wondering whether she should have said yes to this trip, when she is perhaps unravelling. She can't connect to the thing inside her anymore: it feels unreal, a simulation. Mostly she is empty, and scared, and very tired; mostly she wishes she could go to sleep forever.

Nevertheless, Amber appears glad to have Coral with her. She has been uncharacteristically gentle, as if she suspects Coral is pregnant, or at least that she is more vulnerable than usual. Coral hasn't told Amber yet. There was never a good time before they left, with both of them working, and the few weekends filled with organising and errands and packing and resting. She didn't want to tell Amber over the phone: she wants to see Amber's face, so she can gauge how shocking, how awful, the news really is. It will prepare her for telling Topaz, a task she tries not to think about.

Amber has booked them a night in a hotel in the centre of Warsaw. It is near the station where they will need to go the next day to take trains across the country towards the small seaside town where Amber's grandmother lives. Gosia is out of hospital now and at home, with palliative nurses and her family caring for her until she is done, and she dies in her own bed. Amber has told Coral that her grandmother wanted her little dog, Bibi, by her side, and so she was taken home. Coral pictures a fluffy petunia-shaped dog sitting on the bed of an elderly woman, and it pleases her.

They have arrived in the mid-afternoon, and plan to stay awake as late as they can into the evening, to give their jet lag as little chance as possible. Coral is so tired that her eyes keep closing without her permission, though she also has that expansive, breathy feeling in her chest because she is on an adventure. After heaving their bags up the stairwell to the third floor (the elevator has a sign on it that reads NIECZYNNY), they splash their faces with cold water in the bathroom. It is then decided that they need coffee and cake, so they don't just lie down and fall asleep.

Coral and Amber are the only customers in the hotel restaurant, with five young waitstaff standing in a corner near the door, eyeing them. The staff bring cardboard menus with English translations, glasses of water and napkins, and eventually two very tall, very foamy beige coffees in decorative glass mugs, and a large slice of pink cake with fluted-cream flowers on top. Amber wrinkles her nose at the gaudy slice, but picks up her fork and uses it to section off a piece anyway. The cake makes Coral's stomach ripple—sweet things are not agreeing with her this week. She watches Amber chew the cake daintily and swallow.

'Nicer than it looks,' she says, impassively, bringing up a napkin to dab at the corners of her mouth as she does, despite a crumb never ever getting stuck there. Amber applied lipstick after washing her face upstairs, something that would not even occur to Coral. She always wears lipstick the colour of a clingstone peach during the day. It's a brand that smells like talcum powder, or old-fashioned soap. Sometimes Amber seems older than their mothers—neither of whom ever wears a lipstick that isn't red. She remembers Amber in her bobby socks when she was five, and the lipstick dissipates.

'I won't have any,' Coral says, and takes a big breath, from her swollen aeroplane feet up to her oily crown. She should tell Amber now—she needs to tell her, and usually Coral would be stabbing her fork into the cake in order to get at the biggest piece, so it makes sense to bring it up.

Amber's brow is furrowed, and she is looking beyond Coral, presumably at the waitstaff who are likely still staring, because what else is there for them to do? They appear too young to be polite, and there are too many of them. Coral clears her throat, which is uncooperative all of a sudden, and launches in.

'Amb, I have to tell you something.'

Amber's eyes flicker back to Coral and back to the waiters again, then back to Coral, where they stay fixed. 'What?'

'I'm pregnant,' Coral says, too bluntly and too gravely. She doesn't seem to be able to say it without sounding like she is saying she is dying, or she has killed someone, or she is joining a monastery. She would like to be light-hearted, to look whomever she is telling in the eyes. She will try that next time.

When she looks up at Amber, they lock eyes, and Amber's don't move away from Coral's. Amber frowns, and lowers her napkin. The silence chugs around them; Coral can hear one of the waiters laughing from under a hand.

'Sorry?'

Coral knows Amber heard her, but she repeats the words all the same. 'I'm pregnant.'

The silence stops now. There is no chugging—the air has been turned off, has broken down (NIECZYNNY) and needs to be fixed.

Amber doesn't say anything, and then she does. 'Coral,' she says, and sighs, and then nothing again.

The waiter is laughing more loudly now, and another has joined in. Coral imagines they are laughing at her. They must be: there is no other appropriate reaction, she is so stupid, she deserves it, she should try laughing too, she should kill herself.

'I'm sorry,' Coral says, before she can stop herself. She always apologises. Amber doesn't take apologies seriously, though—apologies are just words to her.

More silence.

'No need to say sorry. I'm just—confused? How pregnant are you? Are you sure?'

Coral is nodding, and she wants to help Amber with this, this surprise and the need for a response to the surprise, so she tells her that she is eleven weeks pregnant, nearly twelve. She tells her that she is missing her twelve-week scan, her first hospital visit, to be with Amber in Poland. It hits her, as she says it—how irresponsible this is, how completely unfit she is to be a mother—and she waits for Amber to tell her so. Can she hide herself under the table, her hand on her belly to protect it?

Amber doesn't react as Coral expects her to. She says she is shocked, and worried for Coral, her voice low and quiet, her body leaning forward. She seems to want to ensure that Coral doesn't run away.

Then she is Amber again, and it's almost a relief. 'Why are you keeping it? You haven't thought about an abortion?'

'Yes—I don't know. I know that sounds funny. I knew I had to make a decision but I kept putting it off.' Coral knows this isn't really true. She needs to be more honest with people: they can take it.

Amber is giving her a look that could be described as withering.

'I just got excited about having a little baby, I guess.' Coral picks up her glass to take a sip, adding: 'Like, it'll be hard, but maybe it was meant to happen.'

Fate and fortune do not sit well with Amber, or at least they never have. She is able to tackle life without hopes and fancies, so they don't make sense to her. She doesn't roll her eyes, but she almost does, and Coral hears her tongue click against the inside of her cheek.

'Coral, if everyone who got pregnant thought that they had to keep the baby because it was destiny, there would be even more fucked-up people in the world than there already are.'

The waiters aren't laughing anymore. Coral's stomach (her uterus? the baby?) turns, and the beige coffee foam she has ingested rises to the top of her torso like spume. She doesn't feel anger when Amber is rude or hard. There's no point, she has learned over the years, because Amber doesn't mean to be anything other than truthful, helpful. One day Coral might snap, and scratch Amber's face off with her fingernails, but until then she will take it.

She remembers how long it took her to get used to Amber's unadorned way of speaking, her obtuseness in the face of sensitivity or emotion. Amber is reliable: she will tell you what she thinks, and she isn't scared of anything. Coral has needed this over the years, and she appreciates that it comes with truths that hurt.

'I know,' she replies eventually, because she does understand that life is meaningless. 'Will we go for a walk? I'm too tired to keep sitting here.'

Amber nods, and smiles a bit, and they drink the last of their coffees (oceans) and ask for the bill. They are out on the Warsaw footpath when Amber links her arm with Coral's. It's as if she is saying: I am still here.

2

CORAL DOESN'T SLEEP well after the coffee and the talk of destiny and the walk and an early dinner of pierogi ruskie (lardons, sour cream) and stew at a nearby restauracja. She has been told by Dr Carver that she can have a coffee now and then, even once a day, if she feels like it, but the coffee she drank with Amber in the hotel restaurant seemed to haunt her. All evening, an image of the little thing inside her, poisoned by caffeine and dying, flickered in her mind, as if the thing had been waiting for an excuse not to exist anymore, to never have existed. She didn't tell Amber, and tried to pretend she was fine, just a bit tired, just very tired. When they got back to the hotel room and Amber wanted to go straight to sleep, she agreed, even though lying in her bed in the dark was sure to make things worse.

The thought and the image of a dead caffeinated baby had

looped in her brain as she lay there under the scratchy hotel blanket, also the colour of coffee and with a slight chemical smell. She could hear cars and voices outside, despite the room being three floors above the street, and had tried to distract herself by imagining who was driving and where, but she didn't know Poland and couldn't imagine, and the voices sounded so different to the voices she was used to that it only made her feel more afraid. She had rubbed her tummy softly with the palm of her hand and then lightly circled her belly button with her fingers, picturing the bright fig inside her. After a while the fig split open, and she felt sick, and she wondered if she should wake up Amber, and then it was morning, and she must have slept because she was waking.

Amber appears to be showered, dressed and packed: neatly and ever-so-slightly irritatedly. She tells Coral that it is quite late and that she is going down to the hotel restaurant for some breakfast, suggesting Coral get up and ready, as they need to catch their first train at noon. Amber doesn't ask how Coral slept—she often dismisses these kinds of pleasantries—and Coral is glad, because she wouldn't have had the energy to pretend. She lets Amber go, and rolls over onto her side, her body not quite ready to lift itself up and out from under the covers.

Coral reaches for her phone and googles what caffeine can do to a developing foetus and what kind of fruit her baby will be next week, at twelve weeks. The caffeine could cause a miscarriage, she reads, but this is highly unlikely. She reads between the lines that pregnant people need something, that they shouldn't have to give up every last pleasure in their lives, sacrifice themselves completely, for a baby.

She searches and learns that the baby will be a plum next week: a plum on the smaller side. Coral tries to remember if she has ever seen a plum on the bigger side, but she can only recall the plums that she would pick from the tree out the back of Beryl's house, before her grandmother was moved to a nursing home. The house was in Woodend, outside Melbourne, and the plums were always unripe, even when she waited patiently, as her grandmother suggested, through the summer weeks, for them to soften and reach their potential. They never did, were always small enough to curl her palm around, with their cool sooty skins, resting so snug in her hand. She loved the tongue-curling taste of them, enjoyed in toothy bites on the grass.

If she doesn't rise soon they will miss their train, and so she does, washing her body in the shower, leaving her hair for another day. There isn't much to pack—she only took out her pyjamas and her toothbrush the night before—so she bundles up her belongings and smooths herself out in the mirror. Coral has never dwelled much on her appearance—has accepted that it is unremarkable, occasionally nice—but she doesn't like to look untidy. She has let herself look untidy in the past, and sensed that it moved her closer to chaos.

As she waits for the elevator, before remembering it is broken and starting down the stairwell, Coral realises that she doesn't feel sick at all, not one bit. When something leaves, she thinks, how quickly you forget it.

3

BOBOLIN. CORAL HAD googled the town before they left the hotel in the morning and found that it has a population of 119. This is the smallest population she has ever heard of, and she likes that Amber's grandmother must be included in this figure—that she is person number 119. The name makes her think of snow, of bobsledding, which she has never done (she has never even seen snow before, though in winter you can find it only hours from Melbourne). The town is actually a seaside resort, in the Polish style, and judging by the map it is flat and edged by sea. She decides to hope that there will be snow on the ground when they arrive.

Coral and Amber are picked up from the Koszalin station in the early evening, foggy-headed from travelling so far in a relatively short time. If they had walked it, it would have taken months. Whenever she travels long distances by car or plane or train, Coral wonders at the way a human being can get somewhere without having to move their body. She doesn't tell Amber she is thinking about this as they wait for Amber's uncle to find them. Amber is prone to sarcasm when presented with such reflections.

Amber's uncle's name is Jerzy, and he tells them that they should call him Jurek. He is neither tall nor short, with close silver hair, and has about him a quiet kindness that softens his face. Coral can see Amber's mother in this face, somewhere between the chin and the top of his nose. He helps them with their bags and starts driving, telling them as they leave that it will be an hour and a half before they reach Bobolin, and that there had been a powder of snow that day that might still be visible by the time they arrive.

It is dark, and the roads as they leave the town centre begin to narrow and curl, the trees on either side getting closer and denser. Coral is tired but her brain buzzes, and she wishes she could look at Instagram or Facebook, to distract herself. She closes her eyes and half-listens to Amber and Jurek talking, admiring his musical voice and trying not to worry about whether she should be joining in. She wishes it were daylight, so she could see properly what they are driving through, and Bobolin when they approach. A town of only 119 must be tiny, she thinks, or maybe it is quite large and mostly empty.

They arrive late in the evening at Jurek's house on the outskirts, and he helps them to the rooms they will sleep in. In the morning he will walk them into town to see the dying Gosia. He tells them that her house is only a short distance, and Coral is so tired that Amber nods for both of them.

Coral looks out the window of the room she is sleeping in once she has unpacked and pulled on her pyjamas. She sees the moon, and wonders if the moon sees her, then wonders, just for a moment, what she is doing here. Amber is in the bathroom down the hallway, preparing herself for bed. It is dark out there, with just a few streetlights providing Coral with snapshots of the ground beneath them, where she can see what might be the remnants of snowflakes (shadows, mice). She feels her belly with her hands and notices that it is ever so slightly rounder, tighter, more pronounced. She pats it lightly and breathes in the peace she is feeling, for whatever reason.

4

OVER THE NEXT few days, Coral and Amber visit Gosia each morning and spend the afternoons and evenings with Jurek and his wife. Beata is an elegant woman, with hair the colour of a bush mouse and a prominent collarbone. She speaks softly, with less of an accent than Jurek, and Coral learns that when she was younger she lived in England, where she studied ballet. Coral doesn't often feel comfortable around people, particularly those she doesn't know. Beata has a quality that makes Coral feel as if she can sit within herself.

Amber finds seeing her grandmother difficult, and she tells Coral this. Amber doesn't find much difficult, but Coral can see the strain on her face when she is in Gosia's room, trying to talk to her. The elderly woman is so sleepy and weak that there is no conversation, just Amber asking Gosia things and then giving up and telling her things, and then silence before they shuffle out again, sighing with relief that it's over.

On the first morning, Amber introduced herself. 'It's your *wnuczka*. Amber,' she said, in a voice that told Coral she was wary.

Gosia's face had flickered, then quickly slackened back into an indeliberate scowl, and Coral felt sad that this was their first meeting, these women of the same genes, the same blood—Amber's mother's mother. Too late, perhaps.

Amber cleared her throat. 'I've come to visit, Babciu.'

Gosia's face didn't move at all this time, her eyes (slick, glazed) staring straight ahead at the ceiling, her small hands (tawny, fleshless) atop her stomach.

Amber let a breath out quietly, and slowly told Gosia who Coral was, then talked a while at the muted woman about their flight.

⟡

In the afternoons, they have walked the empty streets of tiny Bobolin, occasionally holding out their gloved hands to try to catch a half-hearted snowflake. There has been no great snowfall yet, and Jurek and Beata warn them that there might not be. The seasons have shifted in recent years. Winter is not yet in full swing, though it should be over.

On their third afternoon, Amber and Coral walk to the main beach, Plaża Bobolin. Before they leave the house, Coral googles what sea they will be looking at when they get there: she doesn't have a mind for geography. She remembers Topaz mentioning the Baltic, and it is the Baltic Sea: her mother knew. She tells Amber, who nods, because she also knows this.

It's too cold to swim—they layer up in jumpers and jackets and scarves and hats—but Coral hopes she can scoop up a little water with her hands.

Outside, it is one of those afternoons that occur sometimes in Melbourne—when the moon already graces the sky, as if it thinks it is night-time. The sign to the beach points them along a tree-lined path that becomes a wooden walkway, the moon sitting between the trees above the water. Ahead, two older women walk side by side in parkas and hats and boots, hiking sticks in their hands. The ground is flat here—so flat it almost tips forward. Coral nudges Amber to point out the women and their hiking sticks, so they can smile together at the unnecessary ceremony of it.

It's windy when they get to the sand, and the squalls mean they can't talk to each other without shouting, so they drift apart to take it in separately. The Baltic is beautiful and wild—the water is layered with blue and steel grey, and there is only a little puff of soapy foam at the tip of each wave. Coral hears its roar below the wind, and she loves it for its ferocity. She would be attending the hospital this week for her first scan if she was in Melbourne. She doesn't feel anxious about this, and doesn't know why. She faces the water, standing against the wind, refusing to surrender. She is so strong and so weak, she thinks.

When she turns, Coral sees that Amber is sitting down, her knees bent and her elbows upon them, her chin in her hands. She isn't watching Coral but she is, in a way, and Coral goes and sits beside her: close, so they can talk if Amber wants to. The sand is cold beneath her bottom, despite the tights and jeans she is wearing. She feels her stomach push against the zip and the button.

'It's beautiful, isn't it?' she says, into Amber's warm, curled-up ear.

Amber has her head in her hands now. There is a pause before she answers, before it seems she is able to lift herself back up so she can move her jaw.

'Yes,' she replies.

They sit for a moment, and Coral feels the wind on her face, her cheeks, trying to get inside her head through her ear canals. When she was much younger, she was terrified of the wind—thought it was trying to lift her up off the ground and fling her about the sky. These days she has a healthy respect for its power.

'Are you okay?' Coral asks. She knows Amber isn't okay. There's that blank field around her that comes when she is trying to deal with something, telling anyone near to give up and go away.

Amber moves her head from side to side.

Coral sighs to show that she is not okay either, on Amber's behalf, and waits for more.

'My grandma's so far away, or something. Pretty sure she's already gone.' Amber pauses, rubs her knees with gloved hands. 'I don't know what we're doing here.'

Coral feels sad that Amber wishes they weren't here, on this beach, together, before reminding herself that this is not what Amber is saying, or at least not the part of what Amber is saying that Coral should be listening to.

'She doesn't know who I am, or she doesn't care,' Amber says, to the sand she is looking down at.

She is so openly wounded that it takes a second for Coral to gather her response. 'She's very frail. I think she might know who you are. Maybe she just doesn't have the energy to show you.'

Coral believes this. When they stand there in the room looking down at Gosia each morning, she sees something in her eyes. It looks like recognition. But she can't speak, and can barely eat or drink.

'Maybe,' Amber says.

More wind, more silence, and then: 'I don't know what I'm supposed to be doing.'

What is Amber supposed to be doing, Coral wonders quickly, and decides that she is doing it already.

'I think this was always what it was going to be like. You're doing what you're supposed to be doing. What your mum wanted you to do.' She pauses, sees that Amber's face has turned towards hers, that she is wanting to know what to do, for real. 'Does it feel okay to keep doing it for a few more days?'

Amber waits, her head cocked, her eyes on Coral. Then she nods. 'Yeah.'

'Poor you, though,' Coral says, insistently.

'Poor old me,' Amber replies.

They watch the Baltic for a while longer, in silence. Together, sitting close, as a barrier against the wind, against the pain. Coral huffs hot air down the front of herself, under her coat and her jumper, to help with the chill. She wants to touch Amber in some way, so she nudges her with her elbow. It makes Amber smile, just a little. She is still able to smile, it seems.

5

ON THE FOURTH day, Amber and Coral wake early and drink coffee together in Jurek and Beata's sunroom. It is mostly windows, and faces a row of empty wooden holiday houses. Jurek told them over dinner the night before, in his romantic voice, that hardly anyone lives in Bobolin, and that almost everyone who does is a proprietor of holiday homes. He and Beata are living here because of Gosia's ill-health, and though they don't share plans to leave after she has died, Coral imagines they have them. They haven't been in Bobolin long, but Jurek grew up here. Beata's smile as he talks of the place tells Coral she doesn't understand it.

A nurse they haven't seen before answers Gosia's front door when they knock later that morning, and whispers hello, as a way of telling them that Gosia is sleeping. When they enter her room, though, she is awake, and her mouth is turned upwards, as if she is smiling. It's so warm in the room that Coral immediately starts to sweat, at the nape of her neck and above her lips. Her body is having a little cry, it seems. It is emotional.

There is a small dog sitting on the covers atop Gosia, near where her stomach might be. It is light brown, with a long fringe and shiny eyes. This must be Bibi, Coral thinks. A sweet little thing.

Amber sits on the chair next to her grandmother's bed. Coral feels like she shouldn't be here, that it would be easier for Amber to take her time if Coral wasn't looming and dripping in the corner. She tries to catch Amber's eye but can't, and then Amber starts talking.

'Hello, Babcia. *Cześć*, Babciu. It's Amber.'

Gosia's eyes remain open, her mouth remains upturned (a little doll), but she doesn't blink or move.

'I'm here again to say hello.'

Amber crosses one of her legs over the other and clears her throat, just a bit, as if there is something small lodged in there. 'So, hello.'

They wait, and then there is a rustle. It is coming from under Gosia's bedclothes, the various sheets and blankets and throws and fabrics that cover her torso and legs. Bibi makes a small whine and shifts herself, puffing out her beard. Gosia hasn't moved before while they have been in the room; it feels promising.

Coral watches Amber watching the movement—her body is so still that Coral knows she is holding her breath. Amber turns to look at Coral and raises her eyebrows. Coral widens her eyes in response, and they turn back to the movement, before it stops.

Gosia's head is moving now, just slightly. She turns from one side to the other, stopping when she is facing Amber.

It is so quiet in the room. Coral can hear the walls. She taps her hand against the nearest one, softly, so that Gosia may speak.

Gosia smiles now, her slack face becoming a walnut. She moves one arm up and out from under the covers, slowly but deliberately, gives Bibi's little head a ruffle, and then reaches the arm towards Amber. Amber reaches back and takes Gosia's hand in hers. Coral can feel her heart shedding like it did last night, but it is not painful this time. She wishes she could creep quietly out of the room, but moving now will certainly break the spell (honey jar, candle).

'Amber,' Gosia says, in an accent both hard and light. 'Amber,' she says again. '*Bursztyn*. In our language.'

Amber nods carefully.

'You are named after the Polish amber stone. The Baltic amber. Found in the sea. Out there,' Gosia says, and pulls out her other hand to wave towards the window. 'We call it *bursztyn*,' she tells Amber again, in a way that makes it known she is deliberately repeating this.

'We don't name our girls after that stone,' she adds. 'But your *matka*, she like to do this.'

Coral remembers something Amber once said about Cecylia and Gosia. How they disagreed over small and big things, how they grew apart in different countries. Coral can't imagine Cecylia holding on to pain, but she knows it's always complicated. She looks to Amber, but her face is still just a smile.

Now that Gosia is moving and speaking, Coral can feel her

presence, maybe even her personality. Gosia seems like she is ready for something, perhaps anything, perhaps death. She is old enough to have lived a whole life, and might be content with that.

Amber is nodding, and her eyes stay fixed on her grandmother, who has finally acknowledged her. Coral feels a rush of love for her friend. It is relief too, because Coral is scared of tragic Amber, and the tragedy seems to have lifted now that Gosia is here.

'Yes, Mum told me. A dark orange stone?'

Now Gosia is nodding. 'Yes, dark orange. Sometimes brown. *Syropowaty*? What is the word?' Gosia pauses, and closes her eyes. 'Syrup? The colour of syrup.'

Gosia's voice and the way she talks is the syrupy part, Coral thinks. Thick, and sweet.

'Open that top drawer there.' Gosia points to a dresser made of glossy dark wood. 'You will find *mój bursztyn*. My amber.' Gosia smiles, as if her amber is a secret that she is finally sharing. Amber goes to the dresser and pulls out the top drawer, sliding it easily (wood against wood). She gasps, and Coral looks at Gosia again, who is still smiling.

Amber turns to Coral. 'Look at this!'

Inside the drawer are nestled many amber stones, and pieces of jewellery dotted and filled with amber. They are mostly a deep burnt orange, but some are brown, and some are almost black; others are so pale or bright they could be orange tourmaline, or fire opal. Coral imagines the drawer handle is hot against Amber's long fingers, her curled hand. Coral wants to pick each piece up and feel the polish of it. She keeps her arms by her side and looks, can almost feel her mouth watering. Amber has never told her that she was named after the stone of the Baltic. Maybe she didn't know, but it seems as if she did.

'Beautiful,' Amber murmurs.

'Yes,' Gosia says from the bed. 'Very beautiful.' She moves her body slightly, pulling herself upwards against the pillows, becoming less horizontal but staying just as tiny. 'Please take some. I don't need anymore.'

Gosia's voice catches at the end of this sentence and she starts to cough. It is a strained, sharp cough that hurts Coral's throat. It doesn't end quickly, and both Amber and Coral move away from the dresser.

Coral tells them she needs to use the bathroom and she does—her bladder is straining below the smooth fig in her uterus. She steps out and closes the bedroom door behind her, glad to be able to give them some time. Gosia's nurse is sitting at a round table, writing. She doesn't look up, and Coral doesn't pause. The bathroom, when she gets there, smells of potpourri. A warm fluffy covering is snug around the toilet lid.

After the nurse has told them that Gosia needs to rest and that they must leave, Coral and Amber are outside again, where it is cold and grey, and there is a light rain falling. The raindrops can become snowflakes all at once here, Coral has noticed, but they are still just big wet plops. One falls on Amber's nose, which is red, and makes her look as if she has been crying.

'Look,' she says, and shows Coral her fist, before opening it up to reveal two orange stones with silver clasps attached.

They sit on her flat palm, burning holes in Coral's eyes, and

Amber tells her to choose one. She could protest, or ask Amber to choose first, but she also trusts that Amber is asking her to choose because she wants her to. Coral looks at each stone—one almost the shape of a love heart, with a silver rim, the other long and hooked, like a seahorse—and chooses the seahorse. It is clean and full and cool against her fingers, and she keeps her hand around it in her pocket as they walk.

6

THE NEXT MORNING, Coral wakes from a simmering dream (damp wrists, wet between her legs) to knocking at the door of her room, faint but insistent. She had been dreaming she was in bed with Jasper and that his limbs were even longer than in real life: he was almost suffocating her with them, the way a big thick snake might. The knocking in the dream was welcome—it meant she could get out of bed and leave Jasper to writhe there while she answered the door. When she wakes and realises the knocking is real, she has to pinch an arm to land herself in Poland before she climbs out from under the covers.

Amber is behind the door. Her nose is red and her cheeks wet; the bulbs of more tears (freesias, spring onions) wait at the corners of her eyes. Amber holds out her arms, and Coral gives her a hug. Amber's body is stiff and warm, and she sobs a little.

Coral can smell her hair—rosemary and citrus, something ambrosial like nutmeg—and soft strands of it touch her lips. She can feel herself waking and realises something must have happened to Gosia.

Amber pulls back and wipes her eyes with a pyjama sleeve. 'Gosia's dead,' she says, and hiccups.

It occurs to Coral that she hasn't heard Amber hiccup since they were small, and somehow they both had a fit of them at the same time, which caused so much giggling and squealing that the hiccups hung around for hours, draining them both of their energy.

'Amb. I'm so sorry.'

To have come all this way, to have hoped for some kind of connection with someone you were supposed to know, and to have had only one day, one hour—it must be heartbreaking. She takes one of Amber's hand in hers, and they stand, and she doesn't know what will help.

Amber is gulping now. She doesn't have much experience with crying, and it seems to have thrown her body off balance. There is snot below her nose and her light brown eyelashes are clumped, sodden with tears.

They walk downstairs together, in their pyjamas and their bed socks, padding down the carpeted stairs, and find Jurek and Beata sitting quietly at the kitchen table. They have decorated their house minimally, but Coral's eyes catch on little objects of splendour—silver candlestick holders on the table, water glasses lipped with gold. These flashes are in stark contrast to Beata. She wears simple, tailored clothing in dark, muted tones, and the same simple jewellery each day: one slim rose gold wedding band

and a delicate silver necklace with a cross.

When Jurek sees Amber and Coral he pushes back his chair to stand, and Beata follows him. They are wringing their hands, their faces creased. Beata moves towards Amber and embraces her gently; Coral hears Amber snuffle against Beata's shoulder. Jurek must have told Amber that morning; he must have known that Gosia had died before Amber and Beata did, Coral thinks, looking at him. He is standing still, his face closed. He has lost his mother. She doesn't feel anything—nothing at all. Not even Amber crying in front of her is affecting her now, and she wonders if this should unsettle her.

She watches Jurek as he puts his hands in his pockets and takes them out again. Hands, at a time like this—what are they for? He smiles at Coral and offers her tea, something to eat. She isn't hungry or thirsty, but she accepts both. Hands are for doing things, for helping.

'Amber?' Jurek asks, to her bent frame still curved against Beata's straight one. 'What can I get for you?'

Amber moves her head from side to side, face still hidden. It is unlike her, this undoing. As unlikely as Coral's current state of apathy. Amber never makes a scene, not so much because she thinks it would be inappropriate, or because she is private, though she does and she is. She never makes a scene because she doesn't need to. Amber sorts through sadnesses and disappointments with a cool clarity that Coral has always been bewildered by, one that Topaz has admired and suggested Coral could learn from. Cool, calm Amber is nowhere this morning. She has evaporated at the announcement of her mother's mother's death, and a new Amber has appeared in the space left behind.

'You must eat,' Beata says, lifting Amber away from her and moving back her soggy hair with one delicate thumb. 'I made coffee cake yesterday; it's still good. It has raisins but is not too sweet—good for a breakfast.'

They sit and Beata prepares cake for each of them, serving the slices on dainty plates painted with corn poppies. Jurek brews tea, and it is dark and earthy. He places a plate of lemon slices in the middle of the table; Coral and Amber watch as he and Beata add lemon to their tea, as well as sugar from a brown clay pot. Coral lifts her mug and holds it near her face. The steam is warm, and she doesn't know what to do about this new Amber, or her lack of feeling about Gosia, who is gone and who will never return.

After breakfast, there is nothing to do. Coral imagines the sugar from the cake travelling to her little baby, her little plum (chew, bite, suck). She enjoyed eating it: feeling each plump raisin with her tongue, imagining one day feeding her child and herself with sultanas from a box, before the imagining felt sinister. After leaving the table to clean and wash, Jurek and Beata have a murmured conversation in the hallway, in a raw Polish that Coral enjoys overhearing. She imagines that Beata is asking Jurek if he is okay and that Jurek is answering that he is. She imagines that they might also be worrying out loud about Amber.

✧

The day shifts and blinks, and Coral cannot concentrate on anything. They leave for a cousin's house and arrive an hour later. The lunch they are served, beetroot soup and dumplings, lulls Coral into a reverie of nothing much at all. Luckily, no one asks her anything. The hosts are polite, but there are other things to talk about and Amber to attend to, who has shed enough tears to be able to speak during the meal.

They watch television in the afternoon, and Coral drifts off on the frilly couch in the sitting room, waking to find herself alone. Then there is more food—cabbage rolls, potato salad choking with mayonnaise, oily herrings spotted with onion, smoked cheese made from sheep's milk—and vodka. Coral piles her plate and sips a small shot glass of the clear liquid, chews at some black bread. The vodka makes her head feel like it might pop off, so she stops sipping and gulps a large glass of water, not wanting to want more. The little thing inside her needn't be drowned in alcohol now—she has managed to stay off it so far. A pickled plum, to birth a pickled plum: it would be a tragedy.

After this, a woman with long, pink clacky nails and bleached hair offers her orange juice, perhaps noticing that she is not drinking the vodka like everyone else. As Coral sips it, she feels the liquid travel down her throat and into her torso, and imagines it is covering the plum with an acidic sheen. The orange juice tastes good—clean and tart, the way she likes it—but it doesn't feel good to imagine what it could be doing to the thing inside her, even though orange juice is perfectly safe for pregnant women and she knows this, has looked it up online.

Coral moves her chair a little closer to Amber's and speaks to the tablecloth. 'Do you think orange juice is safe?'

Amber is in the middle of a glass of vodka, and turns to her with vague eyes.

'For the baby? Because it's acidic?' Coral says.

The vague eyes blink, and Amber places the glass down. 'Orange juice?'

'Yeah.'

'It's safe.' There's nothing in Amber's voice when she says this, and Coral hopes she will tell Coral she is being ridiculous, so she can curl around Amber's certainty when she has a worry like this again. Amber just eyes the glass in Coral's hand and raises one eyebrow slightly.

✧

Jurek drives them home in the evening, back past fields edged with triangle houses, and only a few other cars, their headlights like the eyes of animals in the dark. Coral can't remember what day of the week it is, though it feels like a Sunday. She watches Amber sleep, exhausted from grief and family, as the car rolls towards Bobolin. They arrive quickly, and Coral sees the moon in the sky, just a white dot, and she helps Amber inside to climb the stairs. She is a zombie, and lets Coral take her shoes and socks off and slide her into bed, pulling the blankets up around her chin as if she is a little child.

It isn't until Coral lies down in her own borrowed bed, exhausted but eyes open, mind clicking, that she starts to feel something in the area of her body that she has always been told contains her heart. It is as if the top layers of the red organ have started to drop, and it is so painful that she starts to cry. She doesn't think about Gosia, and then she does, and she feels so sad that the old woman's life is over. It feel unbearable, all of a sudden, to understand that everyone will die, to think of all the ways that Gosia surely strived and dreamed and loved. Coral lets her heart wail and wail, and then she is sleeping.

7

NOW THEY ARE in Gdańsk. The last days in Bobolin that would have been spent getting to know Gosia were taken up with seeing family, planning Gosia's funeral and attending it. There were hundreds of mourners in black-lace outfits and a long ceremonial wake (so much food, so much vodka). Jurek and Beata wanted them to stay in Bobolin until they had to leave for the airport, but Amber decided she was stifled. Saying goodbye to Jurek and Beata, they left for Poland's seaport city.

It is early spring and the school holidays, and there are families everywhere. The hotel they are staying at is in the centre of Gdańsk and five storeys tall. It seems as if every room is full of gangly teenagers and their long-suffering parents, in their mid-forties or early fifties: hair thinning, eyes crowed. It wouldn't be obvious to any of them that Coral and Amber are not on holiday, but rather at the end of a sad pilgrimage.

Amber has been quieter since Gosia died, in a way that could be reverential. She suggests they find a jewellery shop to buy chains for the pieces of Baltic amber Gosia gave them, and they head for Ulica Mariacka, a street of amber sellers. While they walk, Coral asks Amber whether she is missing Micah. They have barely spoken about him since leaving Melbourne, despite Amber making her daily phone call, and Coral is curious to know whether Amber needs Micah as much as Micah seems to need her.

'I am, a bit,' Amber answers, as if she didn't really expect to, as if he is a painting you take off the wall that has been there so long you immediately decide to hang it up again.

Coral loves Micah, and is glad to hear that Amber still needs him. She knows that Amber only sounds surprised because Amber sits so often on her own within the world, not needing to reach out, not needing anything, when really she should and she does. Coral wants Micah to stay in their lives forever: his small feet standing just to the side of a scene, ready to take stage directions from Amber, whom he seems to regard with a healthy awe.

'I wish he'd met her,' Amber says.

Micah had been unable to get the time off work at such short notice—he manages a team at an environmental-engineering company, and they need him too. Coral suspects he could have forced some time off, but Micah doesn't force things, and Amber wouldn't have wanted him to fuss.

When Coral met Micah, after he and Amber had dated for a few weeks, she was surprised to find him so mild and pleasant, so kind. Amber had previously been drawn to large, brutish men who never quite met your gaze, but Micah seemed to want to look into your eyes, in order to truly know you.

Coral nods, and makes some sounds to show how much she can imagine Amber must wish this, that Micah could have witnessed the treasure that was her grandmother.

'He'd love it here too,' Amber says, gesturing at the street they are walking along: Ulica Długa, Gdańsk's Long Street. It is lined with evenly spaced tall, slim buildings in different colours—pale pink, baby blue, lemon butter, licks of brown. The buildings are carefully planned and stand perfectly side by side, with nothing between them. They must have four or five levels, and are finished at their tops in romantic slopes and steeples.

'No internet. I'll have to follow the little blue circle as we walk,' Amber mutters.

Amber is always the navigator whenever she and Coral attempt a journey. Whomever Coral is with is always the navigator, even if it is Ruby or Topaz, who have both been known to get muddled. Coral offers, but no one ever takes her up on it, as if they know instinctively that she would only lead them in circles. Once, when she was younger, she left school and turned the wrong way to walk home. She only realised when it started to get dark and nothing looked familiar.

They are nearing a wide building that divides the street in two. Amber tells her that this is the Green Gate, and they need to walk through one of the four small archways and turn left, towards the amber street. Coral admires the brickwork as they near the opening—she thinks of those who placed these bricks on top of each other, and how careful they would have had to be, day after day. She wants to write something about bricklayers, the ones who were alive in Poland when city gates were built. She won't, though.

⟡

Coral's thoughts return to the thing growing inside her. It is the size of a plum. 'Little Plum,' she says, without moving her lips, 'Little Plum, I love you.' She wants to love it, the little plum, though she can't think of it as what it is becoming quite yet—a baby, and not just a piece of fruit. If she thinks about it as a baby, a soon-to-be baby, her mind conjures something falling on her and flattening her out, killing her and the baby instantly, or someone jumping out from in front of her and stabbing her in the stomach, right at the place where her womb is full.

These thoughts are intrusive, and she has had them all her life, though they are nothing like they were when she was younger. She used to imagine hurting herself or someone else, or being hurt by something or someone, almost every minute of every day (what if I stabbed them in the chest, the chest, the eyes, the eyes, the chest; what if I jumped and pulled them with me, what if I pushed them first) until she was prescribed medication and taught what the thoughts actually were, why they happened, what she could do about them. She didn't want to hurt anyone or herself, not really, but she compulsively imagined it occurring, as if imagining it could control it, could stop it from happening. The thoughts are a coping strategy, and sometimes coping strategies bleed out.

When she had told Topaz, desperate to know if it happened to other people too, her mother had been mystified, and perhaps not concerned enough. It was only when she told the school counsellor, a few years later, when she was so tired from all the things she had to do each day to make sure the thoughts didn't come true, that her pain was taken seriously and she was able to get treatment.

It doesn't help to worry about the thoughts (stop, stop, stop). That is like shooting a second arrow, she knows: worry about worry equals more worry. She has to keep breathing through the thoughts, and keep hoping calm will come when the little plum is born.

✧

As if she can hear what Coral is thinking, Amber stops to look at the map on her phone and turns to look at her. 'How are you feeling?' she asks, nodding at Coral's stomach, which is a little rounder and more firm than it was even a week ago. 'The baby?'

'Good,' is Coral's automatic reply. She won't tell Amber that her mind feels vulnerable—that will only make it more so, in a superstitious sort of way. She smiles as wide as she can without it becoming improbable. 'The baby is growing, I think.' She laughs, as if to say: of course the baby is growing.

Amber raises her eyebrows slightly, as if to say it is not a laughing matter. 'How are you feeling?' she asks again, as though Coral did not just say she was good.

'I'm okay, really.'

Amber holds Coral's gaze until she seems satisfied, then nods and turns back to the phone.

They settle back in to a walk, side by side, and soon reach

Ulica Mariacka. There is a faint smell in the air—it seems to permeate every part of the city they pass through—that reminds Coral of swimming in the sea. She knows they are near the ocean, that Gdańsk is a port city. The air feels fresher too, and crisper (if air can feel crisp, if air can smell of sea).

Ulica Mariacka is narrow, and meant for walking. Each shop along it is a jewellery shop specialising in amber. They have been recommended a place owned by an old friend of Beata's. Beata told them about the certificate that should be displayed in the window of an amber shop, to show that the amber is Baltic, and warned them about the shops that do not display it. Coral wonders what might be sold in place of amber, and whether it would be obvious to the trained eye (real amber floats in salt water, while fake sinks). She is looking forward to hanging the seahorse shape around her neck.

When they find Beata's recommendation, it looks exactly the way Coral thinks it should, with its basement below and steps up to a glass door, lights on inside. There is a wooden box on legs out the front, tastefully filled with select pieces, so that passers-by can take a look before they decide to commit to walking up the stairs. Its name, GOLD OF THE NORTH, is displayed in bold, serif letters above an awning.

Inside, it is warm and quiet. They are greeted by a woman who stands behind a low counter, her face smiling and open.

Amber moves forward, leaving Coral behind. She tells the woman that she is Beata's niece, that they have come to say hello, and that she hopes the woman can help them choose some chains for their pieces of amber.

'Ah! Beata and Jurek's niece! Amber! The perfect name!'

She tells them that her name is Klara, and suggests delicate sterling-silver chains for each piece. The chain she gives Coral feels slinky on Coral's palm and against her fingertips.

Coral stands in front of one of the long mirrors and threads the chain through the clasp at the top of her piece of amber, fastening it at the nape of her neck and letting it drop. The amber lies on her chest, cool and beautiful.

8

THAT NIGHT, CORAL falls asleep with the amber stone around her neck, and dreams that she is drinking wine very fast and killing the thing inside her. In the dream it feels as if this is what she was always going to do, and the rush of the alcohol in her chest and fingers is all she can think about. She is drinking at a dark bar and can barely see the faces of those she is talking to. When she tells them she is pregnant (necking a glass of white) they are horrified, and she wakes with a start, her back wet with sweat, her arms numb, her body limp but upright. She whimpers as softly as she can to let some of the terror out, while not waking Amber, who is sleeping in the other single bed in the room, close by, and lies down again, against the sodden sheet, placing both hands on her stomach in order to calm herself.

The dream is scary because Coral knows how true it could

become if she falters. She loves to be drunk and she loves to ruin things, in her own quiet way. It has always been an option, to drink too much and numb herself and be the person she isn't when she is sober—bold and electric, loose. Topaz has always said that she thinks Coral secretly keeps herself close to the edge. Coral has never understood what this edge is but she sees it and it feels good when she pretends she isn't scared of it. Now, she knows it can't be an option anymore, to get drunk and lose herself. That she knows it can't be doesn't mean that it no longer is.

She gets up and writes in her dream diary before dressing herself for breakfast. She has a ritual lately when she records her dreams—she places a small strawberry quartz stone by her notebook. The strawberry quartz is the stone of remembered dreams, and she bought this one from the witch shop in the old Nicholas Building in Melbourne.

Amber is still sleeping, sprawled in a way she never is when she is awake. Coral moves quietly around the room, gathering what she needs (money, book, shoes) and then walks slowly down the stairs to the breakfast room.

The hotel has a buffet, and Coral wants to eat everything. If she can't get drunk, she can make herself numb with food. She takes four croissants on two plates and spoons a large glob of plum jam (*powidła* is handwritten next to it, on a little cardboard sign) and a ball of butter onto one of them, along with slices of ham and pork that looks like salmon (*lososiowa*), slices of brown and yellow cheeses, and a pile of crimped biscuits. The coffee machine makes her a fluffy latte that tastes like burnt toast, and there are cold jugs of grapefruit and blackcurrant juices to pour from.

After Coral has filled one of the croissants with ham and cheese Amber arrives at the table. Her clear face has faint roads of sleep mapped across it and she yawns twice as soon as she sits down, then lifts herself up. She brings back a glass of black coffee and a plate of sliced honeydew. 'I'm not hungry,' she tells Coral, and yawns again.

Overeating is much more enjoyable for Coral when she is alone, and she had planned to take next scrambled eggs and bacon and bread, a sweet cinnamon plait. She will still do it—her body is primed for it now, and won't be satisfied otherwise—but she knows that Amber will be perplexed, for she has never needed to medicate with anything, doesn't seem to have something inside her that is empty and needs to be filled. Coral can't imagine living without a gaping hole at her centre, though she is starting to wonder whether a baby could fill it up.

'I am!' Coral says, and uses a butter knife to crudely cut another of her shiny croissants in two, spreading butter and thick plum preserve across its scalloped insides.

Amber is looking at her now, at something just below her face. Coral is still wearing the amber stone shaped like a seahorse—she doesn't want to ever take it off. It's hot in the breakfast room, and the cool of the stone is pleasant against her skin.

'You're wearing the necklace,' Amber says, and smiles. 'It suits you.'

9

BEFORE LUNCH AT a cafe that plays romantic Polish pop (*We danced as if the time had died*) and serves soggy square pizzas and towering iced teas, they walk slowly up one side and down the other of the main street of Gdańsk, letting the beautiful architecture and the holidaymakers amuse them.

Coral has noticed that she places a hand on her stomach when she walks now, for no legitimate reason. The foetus app on her phone says the thing is still a little plum, and she is making herself wait to see what it will be in two days, when the calendar clicks over into week thirteen of the pregnancy. She is obsessed with all of it, and the way she can actually feel her body changing. She thought her body might change like a plant—never when you're looking at it, never in the light—but it's happening publicly and openly, and it makes her feel like a different kind of person.

Amber wants to see some Polish art and Coral feels as if she should want to see some Polish art, despite really just wanting to go back to the hotel room and lie on top of her bedcover like a starfish on an ocean stone, so they decide to make their way to the Gdańska Galeria Miejska, where they can see contemporary Polish paintings and sculpture. Coral is unsure whether her legs will carry her there, but they do, and it is good to be inside a clean, white, roomy space where the only expectation is that you witness the creative production of others. There are many rooms; they are told by a friendly attendant that they can take them in whatever order they like—there is no rhyme to the layout.

Amber likes to look at art alone, and Coral doesn't really mind either way, so they split up immediately, without conferring. Coral finds herself in a room with a big window and lots of drawings on pieces of paper of varying sizes pinned up all over the place. It appears to be deliberately chaotic, and she doesn't quite know how to tackle the walls: left to right, right to left, middle to edge to middle to edge, or something else.

She takes a moment to walk over and stand in the sun shining through the window onto the gallery floor. It feels so warm and blessed, somehow, to be there in that sun patch. She keeps standing, with her hands on her belly, and says hello under her breath to the warm little plum inside. She stands until she starts to feel too warm, almost crisp, and then she opens her eyes and shakes out the sleep her body wants and turns back towards the drawings. She will start at the left side of the wall closest to the arch that leads to the next room and work her way along, looking at each piece of paper properly.

Coral likes unspoken patterns, and rules for ways of being. She likes to show art respect too, for its holiness.

The name of the artist who has drawn all these intricate miniature worlds is Emilia Bartkowska. On a small white plaque near the entrance to the room there is a critic's summary of the work, and of Emilia's artistic background: Coral reads it slowly, trying to lodge it in her brain before she embarks on the tour. Bartkowska has chosen to call the exhibition *Na Jagody*, 'Picking Berries'. It is the title of a book written long ago by another Polish woman, the summary says. Coral reads on: *Vegetation is lush, running wild and strongly embedded in the drawing frames. The trees and flowers always have roots and seem to suck out all their vital juices from the paper…*

She will look for the trees and flowers in the drawings, knowing that they have sucked the paper dry.

Coral moves to the art, and takes her time with each piece, trying to see and understand each intricate drawing—so beautifully messy and black, or colourful. There is a small child in most of the drawings, sometimes wearing a little bell-shaped hat, often bigger and closer than the spooky creatures and trees in its surroundings. The child has bright red cheeks and looks scared or sad or something else Coral can't quite name. There are birds and ghosts and gremlins and round blueberries; white, elegant, hooded flowers and red trees, with devils hiding just behind and to the side of them. It gives her the impression that she should be unsettled, but she only feels curious.

A drawing catches her eye up ahead. She doesn't move straight to it, making herself look slowly at the pieces that precede it before she takes it in properly, but it has distracted her, and the other drawings before it don't make an impression. Once she is standing in front of it, she feels a shiver trickle down her spine and land at the small of her back. The shiver is blue, the colour of spinal fluid, and it pools cold inside her.

A small person (a little creature) sits in the middle of the piece of paper, with their legs in front of them, one stretched out and one crossed in, heel towards buttock. They have been drawn in what looks like ink and paint and crayons, in a grey khaki, a royal blue, a red, an orange and a thick, chalky white. The white has been slapped around the head of the creature, like an angelic aura or off (sour) milk. From the frown on their face, they seem to be disgruntled, or perhaps bored or rageful. There is something animalistic about the face: it is small, scrunched, with a red, ripe nose that resembles a snout. It appears as if they are wearing a dress with a sweetheart neckline and turrets of coloured material below its bodice, as well as a blue and white headdress.

Coral stares at the drawing for so long that her eyes lock, and when she realises this she huffs her lips a bit to get her circulation going, and to exit her from whatever the drawing has beckoned her inside of. She is very sad now, and doesn't know why; her heart is pulsing faster than usual and she feels what might be a flutter (a syncopated beat). She should sit down, if there is a seat in this place where everyone walks and stands. She needs to turn away from the drawing but she doesn't want to leave the little creature alone on the wall, with all the other unworldly little drawings, all on their own separate sheaves, desperate to be acknowledged. It is as if the drawing has reached out with one of its hands, through her chest, to grasp her heart. It feels just as confusing and painful as it would if someone had punctured her lung with their fingers.

'Hi,' Coral hears from nearby.

She rips herself away, blinks her eyes a few times and sees Amber, human and usual, now in the room with her, and smiling in her way. Coral takes a backwards step, away from the drawing, and stumbles over one foot slightly. As if she is drunk—and she would like to be drunk, to take this clanging-anxious-eyes-sick-shaking-glass reaction away.

'Oh, hi!' she says, in a small voice that is dislocated, though to Amber the voice might sound normal. She can't tell, due to a clot that seems to have formed between her eardrums and the air around her.

'I'm hungry. Want to see if they have a cafe?'

Coral nods, though she won't eat anything. It won't go down, and she wants to stay close to the drawing. The creature in the dress in the drawing wouldn't eat at a cafe. It would know what a cafe was but it would eat from the ground of the forest—bark and leaves—and would have a stomach filled with undergrowth. Maybe she can order a salad, so she will also be eating something vegetative.

She moves to join Amber, with one look back.

10

CORAL CANNOT STOP thinking about the creature in the drawing at the gallery. Even when she is not actively thinking about how the drawing made her feel (remorseful, for something she hasn't yet done; alive, as if she has never lived), it splinters her mind, attacking her other thoughts and leaving her breathless.

She wishes everything was back to normal and she was waking up to get ready for work in Melbourne—that she had a day ahead of writing an article about a man who had been jailed for killing his wife and burying her deep on a desolate beach, and drinks with Ruby afterwards, somewhere she could slurp them quickly and rant about what is wrong with the world. Instead she wakes up in Gdańsk, in a narrow bed in a hotel room a few storeys above the ground, across from Amber, who is still sleeping.

It is so early that she can hear streetsweepers outside on the cobblestones; the sky out the window is spooky with long, bearded clouds. She needs to wee, and her stomach feels bloated—because she is pregnant, she remembers, the shock not unpleasant but always resounding. The creature looms as she lifts herself up quietly out of the bed and pads across the carpeted floor to the bathroom. In the mirror her face is blurry, the edges smudged, and she can see a chalk aura encircling it, like the one the creature had in the drawing—sickly against the cream-coloured paper.

It's just a fixation—they come sometimes, especially when she is tired or hormonal. She has been tired and hormonal for the past twelve weeks, though the fatigue might be lifting. In place of that thick feeling of wanting to go back to sleep is the grizzle of heartburn above her breasts, making her want to cough or rub her chest, though she knows this won't shift it. She has read that the tiredness can lift at the beginning of the second trimester, and that's where she is now, as far as she knows. She has also read that her heart might start to burn now and not stop until the baby is out. It could be the pregnancy, or it could be the little creature in the dress from the drawing setting fire to her chest.

After attempting meditation with her legs elevated on a pillow, trying to concentrate on the sensation of her breath as it enters and exits her nostrils, Coral gives up and watches out the window. She tries to imagine where each person she sees is going, and tells the little creature to get out of her head when they pop up, over and over again. She taps the edge of the bedside table and shrugs and blinks, but the creature keeps coming.

After Amber wakes, and they shower and dress and leave the hotel, Coral realises she needs to wee again. It's too late and she can't face climbing all the stairs back up to the room, so she asks that they go somewhere for breakfast, at a cafe where she can order a hot chocolate and relieve herself. Amber seems impatient—there is something tight about her shoulders and her mouth—but Coral doesn't care. Worrying about whether Amber is annoyed suddenly feels like a waste of energy. She would rather focus on the little plum, and enjoy something warm to drink.

They find a *cukiernia* with seating, and order mugs of chocolate and a plate of little fold-over pastries filled with apricot preserve and finished with icing sugar. Amber's body is still tight; Coral notices that Amber is watching her out of the corner of one eye, as if she is trying to make sense of something. It feels freeing, in a way, just to sit there and not sacrifice herself to try to soothe someone else by asking Amber what might be wrong. She wonders how long she can last—and then Amber speaks.

'Are you going to let Jasper see the baby?'

This sounds like a pointed question, but Coral lets the pointy end go and tries to answer openly. It takes a moment for her to know what to say—she hasn't thought about Jasper as the baby's father much at all, even though she knows she will have to.

'Yes, I am,' she says, and it is now true. She tells Amber that she doesn't know when she will tell him that she's pregnant, though.

'Shouldn't you tell him soon? Doesn't he have a right to know?'

It is as if Amber has been preparing for battle and has taken all her weapons out in case she needs them. Coral doesn't have any weapons on her, and she doesn't want to fight—she never does. Amber should know this by now, and it feels faintly sad and disappointing that she wants to have this battle, and over breakfast, at the end of their trip.

Coral sighs, and wipes her mouth to make sure she doesn't have icing-sugar lips. 'I guess he does.'

Amber nods, then looks puzzled, as if she is expecting more, as if she wasn't expecting it to be so easy.

They sit and look at the plate of sweet things between them, the splutter of the coffee machine in the background. Amber brings her chocolate to her mouth and Coral copies her, to show they are not so different, that they both believe fathers have rights (though not as many as mothers). She doesn't know why she feels like she has to align herself with Amber, or with anyone, really. Maybe it has something to do with Topaz being the way she was when Coral was younger—expecting compliance, overreacting when there was something like protest from her little daughter. Coral doesn't like to be told that she has angered someone or disappointed them. It feels scary, because she never really knows how they will react in return.

'I just don't know about him,' she tries to explain, properly, for the first time. She *doesn't* know about Jasper—there is something about him that raises the hairs on her arms ever so slightly. It might just be that she doesn't actually know him very well, and that he has changed her life, without lifting so much as a finger, really. 'Something about him makes me uneasy.'

She has said it, and it is now true.

Amber cocks her head. She doesn't seem to have been expecting this, for Coral to bring forth such an obstacle. 'What do you mean?'

'It's hard to explain. He's too much; it's like he's hiding something. Or he's unpredictable. Or maybe he's not—I don't know.'

Coral pictures Jasper's nature as a garden hose twisted around on itself. If you touch it just a little bit while it's on, it spins out, startling all that surrounds it.

Amber considers this for a while, looking down at her cup. Coral waits for her to disagree, to ask for more information or proof.

'Yuck,' Amber says. 'That sounds weird.'

Coral feels a rush of warmth. Now Amber is being kind, and she is right—it does feel yuck. Even if it isn't anything, Coral has been trying for a long time to honour her own thoughts and feelings, her own reality. Her upbringing and her obsessive-compulsive disorder have made that hard, and she has wondered if people who know her doubt her too.

'Yeah,' she answers, smiling at Amber. 'It is a bit weird.'

She can't really explain how she feels when she thinks about Jasper. She doesn't know which of the times they had sex was when the thing was conceived, but she hopes it was the first time, when she thought he was cute and had some sort of idea that maybe he was just what she needed and that she would fall in love with him.

The second time was danker (dark and damp, someone else's dirt), and a smell like rotting fruit fills her nostrils when she remembers it, because by then she felt a bit wobbly about him: his body, his voice, his lack of self-awareness, or heart, or something. She remembers how it felt where their bodies joined that night—wet and hairy and drippy, as if they were overripe and might make each other sick. She hardly knows him, really, but in the last few years she has tried deliberately to listen to her instincts. Her instincts tell her that Jasper might never be more than a very tall boy.

Amber is eating the last apricot kołaczki, delicately, holding it with just the tips of her fingers. She always wears the same ring, a turquoise stone set in a slim silver band, on the Jupiter finger of her left hand. Coral knows that turquoise is the stone of friendship, and she loves that Amber might not know this but that she is being supported in her friendships nonetheless, every day when she wakes up and slips that ring onto her Jupiter finger, index finger, the finger that represents her selfhood. Coral believes this has helped them stay bonded all these years, except when she tells herself this is silly.

'The baby should know they have a dad? Is that it?' Amber asks after she has chewed and swallowed the last of the last biscuit. She does not talk with her mouth full.

Coral nods, because she supposes this is right. This is why she needs to tell Jasper she is pregnant: not because he has the right to know, but because the baby has the right to know its parents. She'd rather not think about it, if she is honest with herself, but it is coming, all of it, and she is rolling down that hill (or pushing up it) with Jasper beside her.

⟡

Outside it is so brisk that fog escapes their mouths and noses, and Amber pulls her blue gloves on. Coral doesn't have gloves, so she sticks her hands in her coat pockets and stamps her feet. Coral never has the right accessories. Amber always does, ever since they were little, when her schoolbag matched her ribbons and her watch and her tiny earrings.

They have decided to visit a building they saw online, the Muzeum II Wojny Światowej, the Museum of the Second World War. In the photos it looks like a giant glass rectangle, jutting out of the earth as if it has been dropped from a great height. Coral likes to see things she could never imagine herself, to witness something artificially beautiful.

She doesn't know how to explain it, but being inside beautiful strange buildings feels like sex—like being in control of someone sexually, someone you are so attracted to that you would eat them if you could, because you want to possess them, to be inside them, for them to be inside you. She would like to take the version of Jasper she first knew (before he became himself) inside this building. She would fuck him in the toilets, and only let him do things to her after she had told him he could. Thinking about it makes her undies dampen, just a little, and her vagina throb.

Coral would like to have a sex life like this; maybe after she gives birth and she feels like it, she can try to. She has only ever had the kind of sex she has really wanted with men she doesn't care about at all, whom she recoils from, because to do the things she wants to do with someone she cares about feels like it could break something. She knows this is probably just conditioning. Women are not meant to be attracted to violence, and in many ways Coral is not. It's the power she wants—the artful power of having a submissive partner—and that she is yet to negotiate with the right person. She will fight against the hang-ups she has been given one day, when she has the energy.

They see the museum as they are walking towards it, between medium-sized blocks of red-brick apartment buildings. Coral stops breathing and Amber gasps. They are floating for a moment, and then they turn to each other with wide smiles. There is not much better than an arresting, unusual building, and a public one at that. Coral finds it hard to see beautiful buildings that are owned by one person or one family. It seems greedy to keep something like that from others, to have it all to yourself.

'It reminds me of the first time we saw the glass-triangle thing in the middle of the Louvre courtyard,' Coral says, and Amber nods.

'Half under the earth,' Amber replies.

Coral and Amber went to Europe together in their gap year. Cecylia had encouraged them to take time off after high school before they decided what they wanted to do. Topaz had been sceptical, unenthusiastic, despite wearing her own travel as a young woman like a locket around her neck. She had once been wild and free, and of the seventies, but she obviously didn't think Coral was or should be wild and free. They had gone anyway, and Coral had written about her experiences in Greece and France and Italy in a notebook she still has. It had helped her to realise that she enjoys processing experiences through words.

The building is surrounded by flat concrete, and there are hardly any people around. It's a weekday, Coral remembers, though she doesn't know whether it's Tuesday or Wednesday. The luxuriousness of not needing to know slows her step for a few seconds; her body is more relaxed after remembering it is not required to be anywhere.

No one stands at the door of the museum: they seem to be allowed to just enter and go where they choose. There are many steep steps in front of them, and these lead down and down, underground, to where the history must be kept.

They hadn't decided whether they would actually look through any of the exhibitions and now Coral wonders if she has the capacity. She studied World War II at university, though not very much of it was from the Polish perspective, and she knows that they may have had some of the hardest times of all here, that Hitler had a dream he truly thought he would realise—a world without Poland, without Polish people.

It is important to know more about it, but she is tired from pushing the creature from the drawing she saw yesterday out of her mind. She doesn't know how to explain it to Amber, but walking down all the stairs she sees in front of her might bring her closer to something she is trying to get away from. Amber might want to learn more about her history, though, Coral reminds herself, because it is her history, because she is Polish, and it might be meaningful for her to know more about the suffering. Thoughts crowd in Coral's mind as she watches Amber just ahead of her, looking at the architecture of the place—its beauty is revelatory, she can see that. She just doesn't seem to be able to maintain a sense of awe.

Amber turns around and smiles at Coral. 'Will you come downstairs?'

'Sure,' Coral hears herself answer.

Maybe she will be okay, maybe she is meant to go down the stairs, maybe she will faint or fall or die, or come across the creature in the toilets and feel their scrawny hands around her neck, which is stiff and sore, she notices now, as if she slept funny, which she did. Maybe she is overreacting: that is probably it. There are always more maybes.

Amber nods and turns back around, leading them forwards, before Coral has the chance to say that she actually shouldn't go down the stairs, in case she does die down there. Amber is too quick, Coral remembers, to be stopped once she has started. Her long hair sits sensibly against her back—Coral loves that hair. It seems like it has always been that exact length, that exact hue. She follows the sheet of it, holding the handrail as she moves herself down each flight of stairs, pausing at each mezzanine, closer to the unknown.

There is no creature in the toilets down the stairs, and for once Amber lets Coral stay close to her as they walk through the exhibits, so she is never left alone with the threats that circle her. After they have apprehended as much of Poland's pain as they can, they walk back up the stairs and outside, gulping the air and placing cold hands on warm cheeks to ground themselves.

Another afternoon moon has appeared in the sky. Amber admits that she doesn't give the moon much thought, Coral that she gives it too much. It is comforting for her to see that white circle up there in the sky, covered in craters. It is comforting to know it's the same moon for everyone, to nod to her friend in the sky.

⟡

The next evening, after a day of walking, they leave Poland. For their last meal they order a stew called bigos, served in a bowl that is a large, hollowed-out bread roll. The bowl makes them laugh and is soggy before they finish the stew, but Coral loves it. The stew is 'very Polish' and 'traditional', according to their waiter, and is full of pork, beef, chicken and maybe even some other kind of animal fashioned into sausage, as well as sauerkraut. Coral savours the texture of each piece of flesh—succulent and veiny—and the taste: ripe and oily and buttery, like a big hot kiss. Amber concentrates on the pierogi and the small, lipped bowl of soured cream they come with, so Coral eats a lot of the bigos. She would like more.

They have spent two weeks here, Coral reflects, as she watches out the window of the taxi on the freeway that takes them to the airport. It is not a very long time, in the scheme of things—this country, its history, her life. She wants to stay, but she also wants to go home, where she hopes a love for the little plum will grow.

Dream

I am a bully in this dream. I tell my friend that my mother is a bad person and try to make them agree. Later, I am out walking, and I see my mother running between streets nearby, as if she is trying to escape me. I yell out at her repeatedly, telling her she can't get away. I understand inside me that she is sorry.

1

CORAL IS TWENTY weeks pregnant, and the thing inside her is now as long as a small banana and as round as a healthy mango. It has been a peach, an apple and a navel orange in recent weeks, but today it feels like it really is a banana, even a big banana (the kind you might share with another person for breakfast). Coral's stomach is finally compensating for it, with a new type of roundness.

She has just stepped off the number 19 tram and is walking around the bend to meet Ruby and have her twenty-week scan at the hospital. Since she and Amber arrived back in Melbourne, she has had all sorts of funny things happen to her body: bleeding gums and a bloody nose; pains so dense and arresting that she has had to lie down on the floor at work, her colleagues politely stepping over her to use the second photocopier; tension headaches in the afternoon; vaginal discharge and constipation, making her feel like the wrong taps inside her are being turned on and off; cramps in her legs at night that radiate into the day.

She wants to ask every person she knows who has borne children, every person she sees on the street with children in tow, whether they have had these symptoms too, even though she knows from all her googling that some of them will have. She wants to ask them how they coped. It feels lonely, sometimes, when she wakes at three in the morning with a burning chest and legs like eels. These are the only times she wishes she might have tried Jasper out a bit more, that she'd pushed through the doubt so she could have someone make her peppermint tea, someone involved in all of this as much as she is.

She still hasn't spoken to him, and hasn't expected that she would have. He doesn't know she is carrying their child around with her, helping it to develop into something that will live in the world, eventually separate to both of them but still connected. She has never liked the phrases 'carrying a child' or 'with child'. They seem to cancel out the mother, or the pregnant parent, turning them into a vessel. Coral doesn't want to be a vessel, though she feels like one today, on her way to be assessed to see if she is still carrying her precious cargo effectively. She has been a vessel that has hosted a disease of the mind for so many years—she would like to be full and whole and enough, to be complete. Maybe she will be granted this wish once the thing is born.

She can see Ruby waiting—leaning against the ledge that circles the front of the Royal Women's Hospital, looking at her phone, strumming the bangles along her arm with a finger absent-mindedly. Ruby is always dripping with jewellery, most of it bought from the op shop and all of it implausibly, preciously ugly. Coral doesn't know how Ruby can be bothered to adorn herself so much every morning, or to scour for it in the first place, but it makes her look intricate and magnificent, and must be nice to fiddle with.

Ruby has seen her now, and slips her phone into her pocket so she can hold out both her arms to embrace Coral—this is how she greets, with every part of her. That familiar smell, of sweet wood, of Johnson & Johnson's, is in Coral's nose now, and she feels those sturdy arms around her. They hug for a long time, Coral getting a chance to breathe in Ruby's hair, and then Ruby pulls Coral back to take a look at her. Her face is full and bright, her eyes open.

'You look gorgeous,' Ruby says, and she means it. 'Beautiful mama,' she adds, and though she means this too, it causes Coral's eyes almost to roll in their sockets. She is not a mama, and can't see how she will ever be, though the position is forthcoming.

Coral has been feeling rather beautiful these past few weeks, in that flushed sort of a way that can happen when your mind is occupied, your body busy. When she looks in the mirror she sees that she has colour in her face, that her cheeks are a healthy round, and that her hair is more of a mane than usual. She can tell she is wearing it well, and notices men and women looking at her more on the street and in the supermarket. Coral doesn't know what to do with the knowledge that she looks beautiful. She has always been nothing more than cute, or pleasant-looking, in her own opinion, anyway.

Inside her head it has been tricky. She has been worrying about things she has never worried about before, things she never realised she was rather laissez-faire about, like germs, and chemicals, and the poisons that are everywhere when you start to think about it—in the air, the water, the soil, the fruit, even in the hospital, where she has been twice now to talk to midwives about her growing tummy and the reason inside. They have warned her about what she shouldn't eat (soft cheeses, raw fish and meat and eggs, rockmelon, bean sprouts, sushi, ready-made salads) or drink (her beloved wine, too much coffee, raw milk, soft drink, energy drink, McDonald's shakes, every flavour of kefir) or do (exercise on her back, tackle or be tackled, box or fight anyone, smoke), and also what she must do (swallow folic acid and iodine daily, rest-rest-rest, relax-relax-relax). It's difficult to follow all these rules without thinking about why she need follow them—because the thing inside her could perish so easily, and it could so easily be her fault; she could so easily be a negligent and selfish mother, and she didn't ask for that.

Coral's obsessions and compulsions have never related to germs or the environment, but rather have focused on her own brain and her internal lack of control, and the ways she could hurt herself or others, with real or imagined weapons. This new kind of fear—of contaminants and sickness—is overwhelming in a new kind of way.

Ruby has been coming with her to her antenatal appointments at the hospital. She offered to, for the first one that Coral had, just after landing back in Melbourne, and now it seems to be assumed that she will attend all of them. There are only a handful of them anyway, for Coral is having a healthy and straightforward pregnancy so far, at least bodily. After this scan there will only be one more, unless something is wrong at this one. Coral feels nervous, in that way where the mind doesn't correlate with the body. She thought she wasn't worried about this at all, but her stomach and limbs are telling her that she is, with slight shakes.

Coral and Ruby are early, so they decide to have a hot drink in the canteen. Coral loves institutional eating places—cafes at hospitals, cake corners at church fetes, collections of mediocre eateries on the grounds of universities. There is something exciting about seeing what is on offer, and how it feels separate from the way food is offered in the real world. They sit on one of the modest rectangular stainless-steel tables and Ruby gets them a chai latte each, generously doused in cinnamon, with a flower painted into the foam of hers and a heart into the foam of Ruby's.

'Yours is a four-leaf clover!' Ruby says.

Coral sees a flower with four round petals, but then she looks at Ruby and at the drink again and she sees the clover. Good luck, she says to herself. Good luck, for her and for the little one, the small banana, the healthy mango, the halved papaya. The little fruit salad. She has never owned much, and soon she will own a child.

They sip their sweetly spiced milks and talk about Ruby's worries, of which there are many or few, depending on how you look at it.

'She's beautiful, but—I think I've told you—she doesn't know how to talk about her feelings,' Ruby tells Coral. She is going out with a twenty-four-year-old woman she met online who had lied and said she was thirty. The woman told her after four dates and lots of sex that she was younger than she had said she was, six years younger than Ruby—that she had felt the need to convince Ruby she was worldly and mature—and Ruby understood this wholeheartedly. She forgives easily.

'I want to tell her everything I've ever felt that I've never told anyone else, but I can't do that if she's just going to nod and smile and tell me nothing,' Ruby says, dipping one finger in her cinnamon foam and destroying the heart.

Coral can't imagine what Ruby has inside her that she hasn't told anyone, but she will keep this thought to herself. 'Do you think she's private or there's just not much in there?' she asks.

Ruby laughs. 'I hope there's something in there!' She places her chin in her palms and looks at Coral seriously. 'I don't know what to do with private people. You're the most private I can stand, and you let me crack you. If she's really private, I'm going to have to bail.'

Ruby rubs her eyes—as if she is trying to get rid of something—and smudges her mascara, causing her to become a panda. It lends a fatigue, a solemnness to her story that wasn't there before, and Coral realises that Ruby really wants it to work with this woman, and is very disappointed that she won't open up. The woman's name is Jorani. She is beautiful-looking: peaked and rangy. Coral has met her a few times and can't seem to understand her from what she has seen and heard. Jorani is an enigma: Coral hopes that she is not deliberately enigmatic, but rather that she takes time to show herself.

'There's probably something in there,' Coral says. 'She just needs to show you so you can decide if you like it.'

The appointment is quick, with a midwife whom Coral hasn't spoken to before. Her name is Laurel, and she is quite unimpressed that Coral has brought a friend with her. A small blot of anger bursts inside Coral at this; she has been feeling more anger lately, and it comes out of nowhere, the way she expects anger usually does. She has squished down most of hers for years, partly because she couldn't be angry with Topaz all the time and partly because she doesn't like the feeling of it—hot, unpredictable. The thing inside her is taking up the space where the anger used to hide, or rest, she thinks to herself, and then she thinks about how much she would like to punch Laurel square in the jaw. That would knock the disdain off her face, Coral thinks, as the midwife applies the ultrasound gel and Ruby grasps Coral's hand, as if she needs her hand held during such a procedure.

It's the first time she has seen the little banana and there it is, appearing without warning on the screen next to the bed she is lying on, in black and white: unsinkable. It seems to be mostly head, and Coral hears murmurs from both Laurel and Ruby but she doesn't care what they are saying; she wants to hear what the little thing has to say, if anything. The head has a face, but the features are all mixed up, and she can't see the outline of a nose or a chin, as she had expected she might.

The heartbeat comes next, and for a moment Coral doesn't realise what the sudden, insistent sound is. It's strong, and quick, and loud—the rhythm is coming from the machine but filling the room. It is alive; it has a heart, and that heart is beating. It's overwhelming.

‘Does it have a face?’ she asks Laurel, who is now less grumpy and more soft, her face lit up by the screen, her eyes fixed upon the little thing, as if it’s the first she has ever seen, rather than the thousandth.

‘Yes, it has a face,’ Laurel answers. ‘We just can’t see it properly today, due to the muddiness in your uterus. But it’s all there. Your baby has a face.’

The uterus, thinks Coral. She has a uterus, a womb, it’s confirmed, and the baby is real and growing in there. It has a face. And her uterus is muddy. She is a river, or a pothole after the rain. She remembers to breathe, and the air she sucks in comes back quickly up inside her like a burp. She smiles, so Laurel and Ruby don’t worry about her, or worry about the baby.

‘So special,’ Ruby murmurs, her bronze face lit up too, by the machine or love.

Coral can see the banana has a little hand, and five fingers, of which the tips can be discerned. It looks like a posy of Buddy Purple flowers. It also has a round belly, as far as she can tell. Something twangs in her heart at the sight of the little round belly. She almost hopes she can be the one to feed that belly one day, before the idea terrifies her.

Around the thing is swishy, like a painting, and she assumes this is the water of her uterus—the amniotic fluid. When the picture disappears and the screen turns black again, Coral bites her cheek to bring herself back.

Laurel tells them she needs to speak with Coral alone, after the gel has been wiped off her stomach and she has been asked lots of questions and she is sitting upright in a chair, having her blood pressure taken. The squeeze of the machine on her arm feels like it will destroy her—it always does. Once Ruby leaves, telling Coral she will be waiting in the cafeteria, Laurel is displeased again.

'I'm going to assign you a social worker,' she says, as if she can do whatever she likes, which Coral supposes she can. 'I'm concerned about your attachment to baby, and the social worker can help you get linked in with what you need.'

She wants to shout at Laurel, tell her that things are fine, to leave them alone, but she knows it would just come out as a whimper, because she is worried about her attachment too, and she does care about the little thing inside her, even though she might not be attached, whatever that means. She has been trying, but nothing seems to make it feel real. She talks to the little piece of fruit at night in bed with her hand on her stomach, but it ends up being mostly words said into the air, words that don't make sense. She hasn't been pretending she is blissfully attuned when people ask her, but she also hasn't admitted that she might not be. Laurel has picked up on something, and now she feels as if she has been caught out, though she isn't really sure what for.

⟡

That night in bed, Coral doesn't try to speak to her stomach. She will give in now, and take the help from the hospital, she decides, staring at the cracks on the ceiling and counting them, because she needs to stay safe. Maybe the social worker will be able to help her with the anguished feeling she has had in her body for so long, the feeling that is getting harder to ignore.

She wants to hope for this, but she doesn't know what to pin the hope on.

She reads a few poems from a collection she bought in Gdańsk, at a bookshop near their hotel. When she had asked the owner to recommend a Polish poet, he had insisted she buy a collection by Wisława Szymborska, 'darling of our Polska', and she was happy to oblige. The verse is translated, of course, and is clear and beautiful, laden with uncomplicated metaphor, and just what Coral needs. She keeps coming back to a poem called 'In Praise of Dreams', and the lines from it that echo in her head: *A few years ago / I saw two suns.* It helps her pretend, momentarily, that anything is possible.

Sleep comes easily: she is so tired. She dreams she is picking flowers in a field of purple. She has an infant strapped tightly to her chest, like a barnacle, and a taste in her mouth that she tries to swallow down. The baby is a penguin, the baby is a penguin, the baby has a face as blistered as the sun.

2

AFTER THE SCAN confirms that Coral is most certainly pregnant and that the baby will be arriving in under four months, she knows that it is time to tell her mother, that she must swallow whatever it is that rises in her throat when she imagines doing so, and charge in with the glorious news. Surely Topaz will be delighted, she tells herself, and then: surely she will be confused, contemptuous.

She doesn't want to tell Topaz at their Italian place. The acoustics are such that everyone in the restaurant, including the easily spooked waitress, would hear her response, and Topaz won't take it quietly no matter how she feels about the news, Coral is most sure of this. She asks if they can have tea at Topaz's house on Sunday instead, and makes out that she has some antipasto she needs to use before it expires in order to convince her. She must remember to buy some from the supermarket on the day—sliced meat and cheese and pâté, or something. She forgets everything lately.

Topaz lives in a one-storey terrace that she has been renting for years. It is in Carlton South, on one of the long, wide streets with green median strips that spike the city; she moved into it when Coral left the home they lived in with Lou and Irene. It is dilapidated in a romantic, deliberate sort of way, rather like Topaz herself, with tendrils of grey hair hanging in her eyes, an ornamental chopstick keeping the rest of it in a bun on top of her head, and her flaking red nails paired with fanciful clothes.

Coral likes visiting her mother occasionally, and can picture a child running around the bright, comfortable rooms, filled with pretty, useless things. Topaz is often changing the furniture around, but the house always looks like it is supposed to when she pauses.

⟡

It is a cold June day, and after a hot shower Coral changes into knitted pants and a long woollen jumper that has always been too big for her. Her belly is starting to show, and she doesn't want Topaz to pre-empt her. It wouldn't work to have her figure it out for herself; it has to be Coral's choice—Coral's choice to tell her mother, because of course she would, of course she wants to. If Topaz twigs and asks her, Coral will have to say yes: yes, Mother, you are indeed correct, I am pregnant, and yes, I was going to tell you, of course I was. But Topaz will never believe her, and it will be a light-hearted sore point forever. Coral likely isn't showing that much, anyway, really. She finds it hard to tell.

She walks slowly from her flat to the tram stop, trying not to obsess. Topaz is Topaz; she will do what Topaz does. It is out of Coral's control, and worrying won't change this, but the worry is caught in her mind. This happens to Coral often. A thought will snag itself on her brain and flap there, against her consciousness, until she takes some kind of action to try to get rid of it. Sometimes it drops out when she isn't concentrating, but mostly she has to convince her brain to let it go, her wind to blow it clear away.

She concentrates on the air that is all around her, that is always there, though more apparent on cold days like this. She concentrates on how it feels against her arms, and how they sway by her sides as she walks. She feels each foot inside each sock, each boot; she pulls her breath up from deep down below. The worry about Topaz drops from her brain, for the moment.

After the tram, Coral remembers to stop off at the supermarket for the meat and cheese. The deli is heaving with choice, and it takes her far too long to decide on sliced mortadella with olives and a triangle of runny Brie de Meaux, though she knows it is worth it, that Topaz will approve. She wants to grab the pink circles of pork out of her shopping bag and stuff them in her mouth as she walks from the supermarket to the house, if only for a distraction, something delicious in her mouth, but she doesn't.

When she arrives, she is glad she has happy offerings. Topaz's face is hanging at the door, as if there is something wrong.

'Hello, Coral,' her mother says, twice, as they sit themselves down on her couches. It is warm, and Coral can smell basil, maybe hairspray, burnt matches. She watches Topaz carefully, waiting for her face to lighten or lift. It doesn't.

'You okay, Mum?'

Topaz rearranges her face into a smile, and moves herself back and up, as if she has remembered she has a body.

'Am I okay?' she asks the corner of the ceiling. 'Yes, yes. I'm okay.'

'How was your day?' Coral asks. Maybe she can get an idea of what is wrong if she hears about it. Her mother is never like this—stooped, flayed. Even when bad things happen, she steers towards the high road.

It takes her mother a while to respond, and then she blinks and seems to snap out of whatever she was caught in. Topaz herself, the usual Topaz, returns.

'Oh, you know. I went for a swim at the City Baths, and had lunch with Patricia and Herbert afterwards, and then I came back here. I've been reading your grandmother's diaries. She was such a sad sack.'

Herbert is Patricia's long-suffering pug, and Patricia is one of Topaz's oldest friends, someone who stands in the corner of many of Coral's childhood memories, and sometimes her dreams. She is a stern person, much like Coral's grandmother Beryl was. A day spent with Patricia and Herbert could have given Topaz that frown.

'I brought the leftovers,' she tells Topaz, remembering them in her bag. The lie comes easily. They are not leftovers; she is pregnant; her mother will soon know this. Something like panic shoots up her spine and then she is calm again.

'I've made spaghetti Napoli,' Topaz tells her, from the

kitchen where she is putting Coral's offerings on a plate, presumably. 'In the tradition of our Italian.'

'Lovely,' Coral replies. She can smell the tomato. She taps the couch as many times as feels necessary, and clears her throat.

When Topaz returns with a decorated platter of meat, cheese and mini-toasts, Coral grounds herself so she can begin, feeling her feet in her shoes and her shoes on the floor.

'I've got some news.'

'Oh yes?' Topaz is busy balancing a smudge of brie atop a small crisp square.

'It's a bit unexpected, actually.'

Topaz pops the toast into her mouth and crunches down, making a little noise as she chews. Then she starts, shifting herself forward and up on the cushion. 'Wine! Would you like a glass of wine? I have some Verdicchio in the fridge?'

Coral doesn't know what Verdicchio is, and she can't have a glass, and she needs to finish what she has started.

'I'll just have water,' she says, 'but can I tell you this first?'

Now Topaz is impatient, which seems like the best mood for her to be in, if Coral has time to reflect on it. She stays on the edge of the couch and taps the fingers of one of her hands against her thigh, waiting.

'Go right ahead,' Topaz says, as if she is gracious.

This is it, Coral tells herself. Just say it.

'I'm pregnant.'

She watches her mother as the news infiltrates—her head and torso jerk backwards slightly, as if she has been in a minor car accident, and her features stretch. Coral can feel her heart beating quickly in her chest and wonders if Topaz's has also been shocked into action.

'Pregnant!' Topaz says the word loudly, demonstratively. Coral has never said it like this.

Coral nods her head. She doesn't want to tell Topaz how far along she is, because it will also tell Topaz how long she has been keeping a secret from her, and how big the secret has grown. She waits for her to ask.

'Who? What!' Topaz is gulping like a fish now.

'I had a thing with someone at the start of the year.' Coral tastes the words in her mouth. 'His name's Jasper.'

She doesn't need to elaborate. Topaz will understand that she and Jasper had sex, that he is the father, that they are not together, that this is not ideal. She watches Topaz and sees that she is disdainful—that her mouth has curled up on one side, that she has crossed her arms over her chest. Coral is sure Topaz had sex with everyone when she was young, that she is quietly proud of it, that it contributes to her self-image, her ego. The double standard is so familiar, it feels soft and warm.

'And you decided to keep it?'

Coral imagines that if others saw them talking, they would think everything was fine, that Topaz was just curious, that none of what seethes under the surface was there. She knows this would be the case for most of the interactions she has with her mother—it is only she who is triggered; no one else, Topaz included, could care less. It makes it even harder to be asked questions she doesn't want to answer, in a tone that can't be challenged.

'Yes,' she answers. 'Obviously.'

'Are you against having an abortion?'

Topaz knows this isn't the case. When she asks a question like this, it is not so much a question as a jab—a way of telling Coral that she can't just get away with it, that she's not so lucky. The jabs always hurt Coral, and they often provoke her. She will keep her voice calm, though. She must, or she will regret it.

'No, Mum, I'm not. Not at all. You know that.'

Topaz doesn't flinch after Coral says this. *It is not my responsibility to know anything about you*, she seems to be implying.

'I don't know,' Coral adds. Though she wishes she wasn't explaining herself. 'I just felt like I wanted to keep it.'

Topaz doesn't say anything, and so Coral adds something, because she always does; she can't just leave it, the way other people seem to be able to. She can't just leave them both hanging.

'The baby. I wanted the baby. I don't know why.'

She can feel tears now, behind her eyes and in her throat and filling her chest. It's upsetting, for some reason (for many reasons), to have to justify the baby. The baby she thought she might have wanted, that she is now not so sure about.

She watches Topaz, who stays silent, and can't tell if she looks sick again, or devastated, as she did when she opened the front door, or whether Coral's own distress is warping her senses. Sometimes she thinks people are suffering when they are not, and the suffering is hers.

'Well. Another silly decision, but it's too late now,' Topaz says, finally. 'I can see it. Your face is fuller; you're bigger under that dress. You need some new clothes.'

Coral nods.

'I'm going to be a grandma.'

Relief, like rain after heat. There is not going to be a fight: Coral can smell the acceptance.

'Yes, you are,' Coral says, and smiles.

Her mother smiles back.

Over mortadella and brie (neither for Coral) and grapes and stale crackers, a glass of yellow wine and water resplendent with bubbles, Topaz and Coral talk about the baby, and the plans for the baby—the remaining pregnancy, the birth, the infancy. Topaz asks if she can be there when Coral goes into labour, in the hospital room as she pushes the little thing out. Coral agrees, because she knows when to say yes and when to say no, and because perhaps it will be special.

⟡

The anxiety of the day still flutters up and down her arms after she has left Topaz and is home again, on her couch, breathing. If this flutter is the only thing she is left with, she is glad and she feels lucky.

3

THE QUICKENING DOESN'T come for Coral until she is twenty-one weeks pregnant, and when it does she thinks she has food poisoning, perhaps from the smoked salmon on rye she had for lunch at a cafe near the office, which had been browning and curled at the edges, and which in any case she was not supposed to eat. It feels like butterflies but she isn't nervous, and then, while she is in an afternoon meeting with Steve and Roy and the rest of her team to talk about the last stories they will cover before the weekend, she feels bubbles popping and excuses herself to go to the bathroom. She googles as she sits there on the toilet seat—*bubbles butterflies pregnancy*—and the first results that come up tell her that the sensations are the thing inside her starting to unfurl, so it can keep growing. She imagines it to be a fiddlehead fern cooking in a pot of warm water, but she won't smother it in butter and eat it when it's done.

Coral sees Dr Carver the next day, before work. Dr Carver tells her that her baby is practising being alive inside her, and that all the little kicks and pushes (the flaps and the pops) are the baby's way of trying out different things they will need to do soon in the air outside her.

She doesn't tell Dr Carver that her insides flinch when she hears it is a baby—that she cannot imagine how it could be, and now only sees it as a piece of fruit or a thing you might find in the bush, on the ground. She hasn't told anyone this, and doesn't plan to. Since she saw the creature in the drawing in Poland and felt it following her around for the rest of the time they were there, her pregnancy has felt precarious. If she gives birth to nothing (a puff of air), she won't be surprised.

She doesn't care much about this. She knows that it's all really about whether she tries hard enough to love and acknowledge the baby—that she hasn't been trying hard enough, and that if she does, surely a love and a bond will bloom. And so she tries harder. The effort of trying, and the thoughts of not having tried hard enough, cause her to start counting and tapping and checking (the front door, the back door, items on her desk, the neighbour's gate) more than she has in years, but it's okay. Mothers have to sacrifice things; she expects she should at least try to sacrifice something. She knows she could be angry that she feels this way but she isn't. Anger only comes when she least expects it.

Coral spends the days before the weekend working on a few stories about horseracing and lottery winners. It feels as though she is working with cling wrap covering her face, and it's not merely because the stories are so boring, because she doesn't care. Her eyes are bleary; if she doesn't harness her focus completely, the words in front of her on the screen start dancing. She doesn't feel she can talk easily—the cling wrap covers her mouth, too.

This has never happened before, though she remembers the days before she got her diagnosis, when she felt stuck inside her head and the words wouldn't come out of her mouth properly. This had been due to a fear in her entire body that she didn't understand and couldn't tackle. She doesn't understand what's happening this time, either.

⟡

By week twenty-five, Coral is forcing herself to call the thing inside her a baby, and when she checks the app to see what size it is, an image of an eggplant greets her. She has had a long phone call with a social worker from the hospital called Pip, who seems genuinely to care how Coral feels about her pregnancy, and whom she hopes to speak to again, and an appointment is booked in for her to meet with a psychiatrist at the hospital in the following fortnight.

She has lunch with Topaz and Amber and her mother, Cecylia, at a cafe in the suburb where Amber's mother now lives, across the river in the south, near the cleanest sections of beach. Cecylia contacted Topaz after learning that Coral was pregnant, and Topaz greeted this with pride and enthusiasm. It embarrasses Coral a little, to know that people are talking about her, and her baby, with Jasper, whom she barely knows and they don't know at all. What on earth could they have to say to one another about it, she wonders. She would rather not know.

It is the sort of restaurant that expects you to place a napkin on your knees and choose what type of water you would like to drink (sparkling, tap, bottle) as soon as you sit, and Coral feels bedraggled and uncomfortable when she arrives, having slept in and skipped a shower in order to be on time. Her tummy and thighs are too big for all her pants, so she is wearing a pair of stretchy yoga leggings she bought once when she had notions of a healthy routine, and they are stretched tight across her middle. She hopes they look like they are supposed to be worn outside the house.

Topaz and Amber are running late, so it is just her and Cecylia for the first few minutes. Cecylia is beautifully dressed and seems to have just had her hair done, but Coral knows that perfect hair is in her genes; she passed it on to Amber. She smiles, and Coral is reminded of the way Cecylia used to smile at her when she was a little girl, and how special it made her feel.

Coral smiles back, and says sorry for the loss of Gosia, and then Cecylia says yes, yes, hmm, hmm, and fiddles with the napkin next to her bread plate.

'Amber tells me you are pregnant, sweetheart?'

'I am,' Coral replies, trying to sound light, as if it is a happy, light thing. She likes how Cecylia calls her sweetheart, or darling, or dear heart. She has always wished Topaz would serenade her like this, but Topaz doesn't value terms of endearment.

'How precious,' Cecylia says, managing to react as if she is just finding out something absolutely wonderful, her hands clasped together up near her pale pink mouth, her eyes smiling. 'And how are you feeling?'

How is she feeling in her body or in her mind, Coral thinks. Cecylia has never been good at talking about what lies underneath her exterior or the exterior of others, but Coral has decided to be more honest when people ask her how she is. She hopes it might prompt some pointers: tips she can use to feel better. Cecylia has grown three babies into three sturdy adults: Amber and her brothers, Tobias and Jan. The sons are male versions of Amber—tall, graceful, somewhat icy, somewhat open to thawing. They all take after their father, Geoff, whom Coral finds unpleasant in his self-possession.

'I'm feeling okay. Apparently the baby's going well.' Coral smiles, for effect, then: 'I'm worrying a lot, though. It's a bit scary.' She watches Cecylia's face for recognition or bewilderment.

Cecylia's eyes moisten. Coral has noticed that people seem to cry more easily as they get older, as if they have lost or let go of the instinct to pretend, as if the emotion won't hide anymore. She notices it particularly with older men—they cry at the drop of a hat, the dawn of a new day, at anything to do with love or tenderness. There must be many years' worth of tears sloshing around inside of them, and the valve that has held them in is ageing.

'You poor love. It can be very hard. I remember.' Cecylia looks up to her left, at the ceiling. 'Goodness, yes, I had a particularly hard time with Jan. He was such a big baby, I could barely push him out. I got so injured. And I was so scared, of everything, after he was born.' She looks up again. 'Before he was born I was scared too, actually. He was my first, you know, so I was unsure.'

Unsure isn't a word Coral has heard from any mother she has talked to. Unsure might mean you weren't sure if you even wanted the baby. She wonders if this is what Cecylia means.

'What were you unsure about?'

Cecylia sighs, then sits up a little straighter in her chair. She moves some of her blond hair from where it is hanging in front of her face. Her nails are manicured, with white tips and crescent-moon cuticles; she wears the appropriate number of tasteful rings on her fingers.

'Whether I wanted a baby. Whether I would be a good mum. Whether we would love each other. I knew that sometimes mothers didn't love their babies, at least not at first. It sounded very hard, and I felt like I had no control over whether that would happen to me.'

Cecylia speaks this as if it is okay to speak it, and it was okay to feel all these things, back when she was younger and pregnant with her first baby, and things were different but also exactly the same. Coral wants to keep talking so she can feel okay too, and she is so grateful for Cecylia's honesty she could cry, or scream, or laugh, or stab the table with one of the larger silver forks that lie near her until the tablecloth rips and the wood underneath splinters open. She has urges to attack things these days when she feel a release of emotions—to get all of it out. They're not intrusive thoughts; they come from the immensity of it all, rushing through her.

'That's how I feel,' she tells Cecylia, her right hand tapping at the table underneath to keep her steady. She does it lightly, so Cecylia won't hear, because Cecylia doesn't need it but she does, and it's hard to explain.

'Yes,' replies Cecylia, nodding, though not as gravely as Coral worried she would. 'I thought you might not be feeling so good. You look a bit sad, dear heart.'

Coral blinks. Sad can mean many different things.

'Does anyone else know that it's hard?' Cecylia asks her.

'Not really.'

'Will you tell someone? Someone at the hospital? Your mum?'

'Yes, I will.'

Topaz arrives as Coral agrees, and she is bursting with flustered stories about why she is late and why they couldn't possibly be upset with her. Coral feels nothing where the frustration would usually be. She looks at Cecylia as Topaz sits down and arranges herself, calling over a waiter to request a glass of vino.

Cecylia is looking back at her. She smiles, and puts one hand up to one ear, curling her fingers and thumb. 'Call me,' she mouths. Coral nods, and taps her fingers against the table underneath, then pulls her hand up to rest where they can all can see it.

Coral can't fit as much food in when she eats at the moment, and she finds almost everything gives her immediate and long-lasting heartburn, so she orders a pea and iceberg salad, and some hunks of salted-crust soda bread. She is glad that the others order properly—Cecylia the battered blue eye with three-times-fried chips, telling the waiter she is 'being naughty', Amber a pizza with four types of cheese on it, and Topaz a steak with béarnaise sauce (one of the five French-mother sauces) that ends up being almost the size of her head.

As Coral eats and listens and answers questions when they come, her brain imagines her hand picking up Topaz's steak knife and ploughing it into her own belly, in front of them all, the blood splattering so far it covers the faces of the other customers, who would have never experienced anything so untoward in their lives. She shakes her head to dislodge the thought, and stabs a piece of lettuce instead. This is how her intrusive thoughts happen—she is not scared—they are often violent and often far removed from what she wants, from what she is capable of. She doesn't want to stab through her skin and hurt the baby. It's just a glitch, and her glitches involve the baby now, because the baby is part of her.

God, she thinks—she'd like to finish off the glasses of wine that sit around her. Amber's is orange, Cecylia's pale yellow, Topaz's the colour of dried blood. She'd scull them all and wave her hand for more before she was done. She'd get that loose, numb feeling as soon as she could.

Instead, she listens to Topaz, who is telling Cecylia how happy they are, how wonderful it all is. Coral nods her head, as if to agree.

4

IN HER TWENTY-SIXTH week, Coral can't sleep very well, and her dreams are like living nightmares that play out in the dark. After she has written them up in her dream diary as best she can, she has a shower and runs the taps cold at the end, as a possible punishment for something she isn't sure she did. She can't quite believe she still has to go to work, but she trudges there each day, trembling slightly from all the wakefulness, replaying the chaos of her night imaginings as she stops in at a cafe to get herself a fluffy drink.

The baby is the size of a corn cob now—it is menacing to Coral that sheaves of her baby could be growing in a field. She remembers watching *Children of the Corn* at Amber's house when she was seven, Cecylia and Geoff completely unaware in bed upstairs, and how she couldn't sleep for weeks without the bedroom light on, for fear that one of the corn children was standing straight up in her closet.

The dreams feature blood and guts and long, glinting knives, and they also feature Jasper, who is in the middle or at the edge of every one of them, looming tall and unnecessary, and her mother, looming short and cross. It's the last week of the second trimester, and she doesn't really know what this means. She does know that she needs to decide whether she will tell Jasper, that her subconscious seems impatient for an outcome. She would prefer to see him before she gets too swollen—the last time he saw her and touched her, he pronounced her ankles 'perfect'. It shouldn't matter whether he still finds her attractive; in fact, it doesn't. But she would like to hold the conversation in her hand, not just have to drop it in front of her.

She texts him. *Hi, how are you? Are you free for a coffee one morning this week? Before work at All Are Welcome? Coral*

It's best to meet early, across the road from her office on High Street. She doesn't want to end up going home with him again, to that sweaty palace filled with dirty dishes and old *Beat* magazines. It is surprising what one will do in a moment that one looks back on and cannot relate to at all, Coral reflects. She supposes that is what life is—looking back at ourselves and thinking: Was that me? Why did I do that? Thank goodness I have changed. I am different now. But Coral knows she hasn't changed, and so she takes precautions.

He writes back quickly, as always. *Hey sure sounds good Tuesday?*

The lack of the effort of punctuation offends her, sending that blot of anger straight to her chest, where it has been so often lately. She writes back carelessly too. *Yep. 8.30.*

Tuesday morning is beautiful. Clear, crisp and hopeful, with a sky the colour of forget-me-nots. Coral wakes early—before six—and lies in bed on her back, placing her hands, palms flat, fingers outstretched, over her stomach. She hasn't been masturbating much: it feels as though her body isn't hers to make feel good anymore, but this morning her vagina feels hot and wet, and the dream she was having before she woke has caused her thighs and pelvis to throb. The dream was a drawn-out sort of dance with a man who was half-Jasper and half someone much more appealing. He had Jasper's hair and height and mouth, but the rest of him was pure and dusky and all-knowing, and Coral melted into him as they slowly swung around together on a kind of dancefloor. She could feel their hearts beating, in the dream, and then he leant down and kissed her. She wanted him to slide himself inside her as soon as possible but she woke up, for no apparent reason, just as he was moving his hand up under her top, to fondle her nipple.

As she remembers the dream, she says out loud, 'I'm sorry, baby,' and begins to rub at herself, finding that perfect spot in the middle, and imagining what it would feel like to have the dream man move his steady hands across her breasts and pull at her nipples. She knows what Jasper felt like when he was inside her, sliding against her, huffing in her ear, and she makes it even sexier for herself with the man from the dream who was more someone else than he was him. She imagines them up against the wall of the vast room they were dancing in, him grunting, her moaning, everything so hot and smooth and wet, and then she rubs harder and harder while she pictures herself pulling him around and pushing him onto the ground, moving herself onto him and then across him, back and forth, back and forth, and finally telling him to pull out and cum on her, because that always makes her orgasm (her in control of his loss of control, the spurt, the collapse making her feel in control and out of control). The bed below her crotch is wet now, and she lies flat like a dying animal for a minute, panting, before lifting herself slowly up to shower and slap at her tingling cheeks a little bit.

Now she hopes she can face Jasper with no sexual tension in her body. She whispers, 'I'm sorry, baby,' to the baby again, and wonders how she can explain that what she did was not about the baby, had nothing to do with the baby, was private, for the baby's sake. She decides not to think about it. Babies don't remember their time in the womb, so their parents can get themselves off without fear, can't they? Yes, she says to herself in the bathroom mirror, before brushing her furry teeth.

⟡

Jasper is sitting at one of the tables outside when she arrives. He is too big for his stool, and is just waiting there, not looking at his phone, not reading, just waiting, and when Coral enters, standing up, reminding her just how tall he is, and how he doesn't know what to do with it, really, though he tries to pretend that he does. Something moves in her belly (a kick or a punch) and she wonders whether the baby knows it is about to be announced to its father. She wonders whether the baby will be tall, or have curly hair, like Jasper, or whether her less expansive genes will prevail.

He is smiling, or leering (she cannot tell), when she reaches the table, and she watches him see her belly. It's not huge, but it is there, and it is not able to be hidden or denied, and she is suddenly very nervous. She should have told him earlier, he will be hurt, maybe angry, she thinks, and now she can't look at him. The baby is kicking inside her still, a little softer but with more rhythm. She makes herself look at Jasper's face. His mouth is slightly open, and he is breathing in air like a frog.

'Are you—'

'Pregnant?' The word is too much, but it is the truth.

He nods.

'Yep,' she says. And then, when his face doesn't move, though he is still breathing through his mouth, she adds, 'Sorry.'

She's not sorry. That's not the right word. There's no word, really. She doesn't have to say anything at all. She's sick of saying sorry when she's not and she shouldn't be. It's not her fault that his sperm didn't know what was good for it, but (she pats her tummy briefly; she doesn't want to curse the little thing) it happened, and she won't say sorry for it anymore.

Jasper is still standing, sort of hovering, like he might faint, or maybe that's just the way he stands, and then he sits down abruptly on his stool and it almost slips and falls beneath him. He places his elbows on the table, and his head in his hands. Coral doesn't know what to do, so she sits too, and places her hands in her lap, politely.

He lifts his head and smiles, weakly. 'Would you like a tea? Or—a juice?' he asks her, as if this is the priority.

'I'll have a coffee, please. A cappuccino,' and when he raises his eyebrows slightly at this, like all men seem to do, she snaps.

'I'm allowed one or two coffees a day. One won't kill anything.'

He nods his head, as if she is his master, and stands.

'And a morning bun, if they have any left,' she says.

He nods his head again.

When he gets back with their coffees, the cups tinkling against their plates because his hands seem to be shaking slightly, they face each other at the table and she looks at the whole of his face. She can see the pores that decorate his nose, gaping, and he has a sweaty forehead, but she would also like to put her tongue in his mouth and her hands down his pants, because something about him is sexy to her right now, like it was back then, like it might always be. When he moves his arms (as he talks, back and forth, up and down) she gets a whiff of his underarms. He doesn't seem to wear deodorant, and she wonders what goes through his head in the mornings, after his shower, before he dresses.

'I don't know what to say,' he says finally. 'How do you feel?'

She has thought about how she will answer this, and wondered if he would actually ask. 'I feel excited.'

It doesn't matter that she mostly feels things other than excitement: he doesn't need to know. If she doesn't say she is excited, she is worried it will jinx the baby and their roles as parents of the baby. She can't tell him all the other things she feels, in case she never sees him again, and he spends the rest of his life carrying around a small, vague part of her from that moment, when she couldn't properly elaborate on all the ways she is terrified, or justify them, or say that it would be okay despite them. She'd rather he just know her as the excited mother—a nurturing parent, an independent woman.

He is smiling properly now, at last. 'I'm excited, too!' he says.

How easy it is for him. Of course he is excited. He doesn't have to do anything, to carry anything, to live with anything, unless he wants to, and even then it will all be separate from him in a way that means he can keep breathing. She wishes he was the one who was carrying their little child around inside, growing the child with his fluids, worrying about what he ingests, preparing himself for the labour and the birth. If he was the one who was beginning to waddle, whose ankles and wrists were beginning to swell, she would be so kind to him.

'Do you know if it's a boy or a girl?'

'No, I decided I wanted a surprise,' she says, and this is also partly true (she has always liked surprises, cutting through the sameness of life, though a baby will cut through this sameness no matter what), but mostly she doesn't know whether the baby will be given the gender of boy or girl because she wasn't ready to face this when the time came to decide if she wanted to find out, and the time has passed, in a way, now.

Her passivity through this pregnancy has not shocked her—she has always been this way, perhaps because of Topaz and her overwhelming bumptiousness, her taking up of all the space so that it was easier to be still than to try to move. One thing that is pleasant about Jasper is his apparent acceptance of Coral's passivity. The other men she has kissed or dated or slept with have commented on it, and it has made her feel like she should be more than she is, that she is not living properly. Jasper seems to acknowledge her and that's that. Perhaps it is because he isn't aware of how others are moving through the world, but she hopes it is because he doesn't want to change people, or because he likes the way she moves: slowly, though not necessarily carefully, her head in the cottonwool clouds.

They ease into a conversation about names, something Coral was not expecting.

'I like the name Forest, for a boy or a girl,' Jasper tells her, in a way that communicates he is serious but shy about it.

'That's beautiful,' she replies, and she means it, because she knows that won't be her baby's name.

'My grandmother's name is Gwendoline and people call her Gwen. Could a baby be called Gwen?'

She shakes her head. 'No, I don't think so.'

He nods, as if he suspected as much.

'I like Flint,' Coral says. It's the first time she has said the name out loud. 'For a boy or a girl.'

His eyes widen. 'I've never heard Flint before.'

'I found it in a book about rocks and stones,' she says. 'I don't think it's really a name, but it sounds strong. A bit magical.'

He takes his phone out of his pocket and starts typing into it, using his broad thumbs.

'It's a name!'

'Ah!'

'Usually for a boy. It means flint rock. Hang on—' he keeps typing with those thumbs. She remembers them pressed into her collarbone, when he dropped his saliva down on her and slurped it up. That was just before he had brought her to orgasm.

'And flint rock is a type of quartz. Brings safety and protection.' He looks up and smiles at her again. Her pelvis lurches.

'Our little flint rock,' she says.

They both smile and then laugh a bit and she wonders what he would say if she suggested they go and fuck, quickly, in a toilet stall. She is quite sure he would say yes, and that it would feel good. The baby wouldn't mind. Mum and Dad having a bit of fun, some pleasure in the house. She looks at her watch and realises she is late for work.

Outside they say goodbye, and then he reaches out his arms and they hug, awkwardly, long enough for her to breathe in his smell (supermarket hair gel, pepper).

'Can we hang again?' he asks, after they break apart.

She says yes, and wonders whether this is the right decision. As she crosses High Street, she can see him rushing to a tram. He runs with his arms in front of him, as if he is trying to catch a ball. She smiles, because she doesn't know what else to do. A yawn comes after that, and she feels the baby kick her.

5

AT THE OFFICE Coral still wants to use her time to learn, and she tackles the assignments she is given with the determination to become immersed, to do good work. She is always tired now, and her anxiety means she has to go to the bathroom to breathe and tap and collect herself often. She's started moving towards the bathroom just to feel the relief wash over her, and she can feel the beginning of the shrugging of her shoulders that she did when she was a little girl coming back, as a repetitive movement that makes her feel calmer when things feel too high and big.

She will tell Dr Carver about this soon. Her medication isn't quite helping her stay grounded, the way it usually would. She doesn't know what she is anxious about, apart from the impending and colossal change she has embarked upon without really choosing to. She supposes it's normal to feel funny, though how funny she doesn't know.

Coral travels by train from the office to the site of a crime that shocked the team when they first heard about it—a mother's murder of her child, a three-year-old called Ivy. Roy is covering the case, and Coral asks Steve if she can tag along. They are solemn on the journey, even though they have known about the tragedy (the horror, the agony) for days.

There has been a steady drone of conversation about this crime in the office since the big papers broke the story the morning after it happened, and Coral doesn't know if she has been imagining her colleagues looking at her belly and then up at her face, with eyes that tell her they are wondering whether she could ever kill the precious thing inside her. There is no sympathy, no empathy for the mother who did it—she is a monster, and that seems to be the only undisputed fact. Coral doesn't think the mother is a monster, but she keeps it to herself. She thinks the mother is a human, surely a victim of illness and expectations.

It's good to be on assignment with Roy. Coral is fond of him and his floppy outfits, his tired-old-dog eyes. He is almost a character in a film—the man who has lived a life but is weary now. Roy asks her how she is feeling, genuinely, and offers her half of his mortadella and sweet-mustard-pickle sandwich. She takes it, and the margarine mixed with the pickle and the meat is luscious in her mouth.

'I'm okay,' she says.

They have just stopped at Heatherdale Station, and Coral watches Roy watching the few people who are waiting at the door to step onto the platform.

‘Okay,’ he echoes, and lifts one hand to brush a crumb of bread from the corner of his mouth. She had wondered if he had realised it was there. ‘And what does okay mean?’

How to explain all the things inside, she thinks, but she can try with Roy. He won’t judge her. And if he doesn’t understand, the way he asks for clarification is gentle.

‘I’m anxious. I don’t know how I’m going to become a mum all of a sudden, when I’m not one now. I don’t feel like one.’ She stops, then pushes on. ‘I mean, I sort of do, but I don’t know what it feels like, so I don’t really know…’

Roy lets the sentence trail off, seems to have no urge to jump in—to polish the moment, or be heard. He’s helpful like that, because sometimes Coral needs a bit of silence in order to have the space to speak what she is actually trying to say.

‘I feel like I’m floating. In a bad way,’ she says, eventually. Even though that sounds haunted, or deranged, it’s true, and she expects Roy will understand. When there are big things on the horizon, Coral’s body tends to float just above itself. She’s been told it’s called disassociation, and that it’s a coping mechanism: her body’s way of keeping safe when the circumstances are too real and could destroy her. She likes that her body does this, without her even having to ask. It does, however, make living and getting on with things hard sometimes.

Roy doesn’t have any children, or a partner. Coral can’t figure out why, because she so easily imagines him being someone’s person, but he isn’t, and he seems tired and sad sometimes in a way that suggests he wishes he was. She has wanted to ask him about it ever since she began working with him but there doesn't seem to be a way of asking 'Why are you alone?' that doesn't reverberate.

Roy seems as if he is trying to forget something, though Coral could be assigning to his life a level of melancholy and intrigue that is more about her than him. Her identification with people can sometimes become all-encompassing, and then it doesn't tell her anything much except that she is too close, so she starts to float again, to get away from it all.

As if he can hear her thoughts (so close to the skin), Roy shifts himself in his seat, clears his throat and says, 'I always wanted a kid.'

She nods, a lot, at the seat in front of her, not turning towards him yet.

'I can't keep a girl, though. They're always disappointed.'

So he is slow like this always, Coral thinks. It's hard to stay beside a slow partner—she wonders if she would also be a slow partner, but has never let a boy hang around long enough to confirm it for her. Jasper might not mind if she is slow, she thinks: the thought shoots through her like subliminal messaging. But she doesn't want Jasper and his naivety. He might be dangerous, in an unassuming way, she thinks, though she could be proven wrong.

'But you're lovely,' she says, before she can stop herself, and then he takes her hand in his and holds it, and she lets him, wants to let him, almost.

It feels nice to know that he cares about her. She wants him to know that she cares about him too. They sit facing the chairs opposite them, the suburban landscape rushing by in pale green and plaid brown out the window, and she breathes all the way down to her diaphragm and holds it there to keep herself still. After enough time has passed, she moves her hand away, to scratch an itch on her face that isn't there. She hears Roy's breath rush out—he must have been holding it in, too.

Coral wishes they could get off at Ferntree Gully Station (the woman who killed her child lived among the silver banksia and the weeping bottlebrush trees; she drove an orange van). She wishes they could find a pub to drink a long cool pint of beer in, and then another, and then another, until she is drunk enough to give Roy a kiss and not regret it, because her body wants something to happen that isn't just the baby. She can't, though, and she can remind herself quickly, now that the bump is visible when she looks down and now that she can feel it moving around inside her.

She doesn't want to learn more about this poor woman who suffocated her little girl with a pillow, or maybe she does—maybe she wants to be horrified. All she knows is that the woman must be suffering intensely.

When they arrive at the house, up a steep hill that twists like a snake, there are a few constables scattered in the front yard, seemingly trying to find out something. It has been five days since Ivy died, and five days since her mother, Sheila, was incarcerated, awaiting next steps in her likely long and cruel punishment. Coral wonders why the police are still circling the house, as if there is something they can find, as if there is something they can do, when it is far too late.

Coral and Roy are here because they are writing a piece that is supposed to focus on the woman and the child—their circumstances, the likely injustices that led to the crime. Neither of them know Ferntree Gully well; Coral only remembers visiting one time, in her early twenties, to see a terrible ska band perform at the local pub with Ruby. They have decided it is worth coming up here to understand a little more about where Sheila and Ivy lived, and the architecture of their existences.

The house is sprawling and dilapidated—it seems much too big for two people, one of whom was very small. Coral believes in the power a big house has to swallow its occupants, and this seems to be the perfect example. Growing up in small surrounds in the inner city, with many other people around her always using the bathroom and the kitchen and the living area and the stairs, Coral was held. If it had just been her and Topaz in a monstrous house like this one, she can't imagine what they might have done to each other. Of course, it is not this simple—a house does not make a mother kill her child. But a mind that chooses to live separately like this can be a mind that is starting to get sick, and there is no help out here, though the city is not all that far away.

Roy is the only other person in her office who appears not to be angry at the mother for what she has done. He doesn't seem to have much anger in him at all, and his voice is frail when he utters either name: Sheila, Ivy. Coral knows that she and Roy make a good team—he has many years of experience as an amateur detective, and they both lean towards the secrets people have, rather than to their own projections. She respects Steve just a little for letting her accompany Roy. She also finds the story scary—if another mother can kill her baby, could she kill hers? It's an abstract question, and she has no genuine homicidal impulses, but she doesn't think herself above anything, really, and maybe this mother was once a confused pregnant twenty-nine-year-old like she is. Perhaps the trick is to reach out and tell someone, before you get stuck in such hell, she tells herself.

They knock on the doors of the closest neighbouring houses, and only manage to speak to one person, an older woman called Joan who asks them in for a cup of tea when she hears why they are there, and whose eyes well up with tears when they begin talking about the woman and her girl.

'She was a good mother, I thought,' Joan tells them, halfway through a biscuit, her mouth speckled with crumbs and her lined face caving. Coral knows what it feels like to have a mouthful of food and eyes full of tears. It feels like everything all at once.

'Trying her best, she was. And dear little Ivy,' Joan says, with love in her voice. 'I'd look after her sometimes, when Sheila had to work at the pub. She'd curl up on the couch with me and we watched telly. She never asked me to change the channel.' Joan brushes away the crumbs at her mouth with one of her sleeves. 'She wasn't hungry or neglected. I would have known.'

She pauses, eyes milky. Then she clears her throat. 'I'm sure they loved each other.'

Coral feels for Joan in her chest and her arms and her eyes and her whole body so much, and so much for the ruined existences of Ivy and Sheila, that her chest hurts, and her stomach rumbles in an unusual way that isn't because of hunger. She excuses herself and sits on the toilet seat in Joan's bathroom, her head in her hands, until the roar of devastation quietens down a bit. There's no point making yourself sick, she tells herself, more sick than you already are.

When she gets back, Joan and Roy are each eating another biscuit in what seems like companionable silence. Coral admires the way Roy interviews—the few times she has witnessed him with a subject she sees how tender he is, how safe and unbothered it feels. She knows journalism often doesn't provide what people need, but when it does, through these careful interviews that are more like debriefs, like therapeutic bubbles, or when a story helps to change some kind of injustice that the world has been accepting, Coral feels proud and good.

They don't find out much else from Joan, who seems to tire after she has eaten her biscuits (Marie, Monte) and told them how much she cared, and so they thank her profusely and leave her, a sadness rolling through Coral again as Joan shuts the door and is alone again, in her musty house with her memories.

It is good to be here, where the mother and daughter lived, in the air they breathed each day, Roy says, as they stand around and then decide to head back to the office. Roy will have to work late to get some sort of draft together—it is Thursday, and Steve wants the piece by Monday morning.

Coral washes around in her thoughts on the train ride back to the city, and sighs and yawns a lot, because she has remembered how tired she is. It's dusk when they hop off the tram outside the Northcote Town Hall. Roy pops in to a convenience store to buy them each a ready-made sandwich. He lets her choose: curried egg or ham.

6

THE APPOINTMENT WITH the perinatal psychiatrist is at the hospital, in a clinic wing that has comfortable chairs and comfortable music playing out of speakers hung in the corners of the ceilings. Coral doesn't feel nervous, but her stomach is fluttering and the baby is punching her a lot, perhaps because it knows that they are going to be assessed and it wants to have a say in the outcome. Coral gently pats her rounded belly and feels how taut it is. She whispers, 'You're okay, you're okay,' to both of them.

It doesn't take long for her to be called by the kind receptionist who told Coral she had a lovely name when she arrived. A kind receptionist can sustain Coral for a whole day, and this one is pretty too, with a thickly curved waist and swooped blond hair and dimples. She wonders whether the receptionist has children of her own, and is sure that she does. There would be three of them, all blond, between the ages of one and five. The receptionist would make muesli biscuits for them, pancake stacks on weekends.

The swoopy receptionist calls Coral's name, then guides her into a small room that looks like a regular doctor's office and beams at her, asking if she needs water or to know where the bathroom is. Coral doesn't need to wee, but she could at any moment—the baby has started pushing down on something that seems to make her bladder smaller, and she is trying to drink enough water, too, so there is more to let slosh out between her legs. The water that the receptionist brings her is in a paper cup, delicate and perspiring. She is thirsty as soon as she takes a sip, and drinks the rest down in a gulp that makes her cough.

The wait for the psychiatrist is longer. Coral thinks this might be how it happens in countries like America—waiting in reception, then being taken to a room, then another room, the doctor appearing hours later, from somewhere mysterious and important, deep within the bowels of the series of yet more rooms that you have been waiting on the outskirts of. In Melbourne she has been used to waiting in reception for the longest time; when you are taken to the next room, it has the person you are there to see and you don't have to wait any longer. This suits Coral. The biggest wait in the biggest room, with walls that are further away and less likely to collapse on her.

She arranges herself on the chair in preparation for the psychiatrist's arrival, but she can't get comfortable, and a thought pops in of how easy it would be for her to hurt herself in this room, or to hurt the baby. There are medical instruments in a corner (to cut open her head and remove her brain?), and a letter opener next to her on the desk that looks as if it could wound the heart in someone's chest.

The amount of blood that would fall to the floor if she stabbed herself in the belly with a letter opener is filling up her mind when the door of the small room opens, and a short, slight woman enters, smiling lightly at Coral with a lined face and spectacles and a painted mouth the colour of a peanut shell. Coral smiles back, and she waits as the woman pulls up the other chair and sits down upon it, placing the notebook and pen she is holding on her lap and crossing her trousered legs. The woman has brought a smell with her: Coral thinks it might be musk, mixed with something else. It reminds her of the walk home from the milk bar around the corner when she was little, biting at a soft but sturdy musk stick. She remembers the pink, sweet crumbly taste that would fill her mouth.

'Hello, Coral,' the woman says, and she opens up her notebook and flattens the pages down. 'I'll be taking notes today, if that's okay with you. Just in case you wonder what I'm doing. It's so I can remember the main points we discuss, for next time.'

Coral can smell the fresh pages of the notebook now, and the mixture of the musk and the paper and the something else is agreeable. She nods and smiles again, and watches the woman take the lid off her pen and secure it to the pen's end.

'How are you today?' the woman asks. She wants to know, and has her pen poised, but Coral doesn't really have it in her to explain how she is, to ask herself how she really is, so she can then try to put that into words.

'I'm well, thanks,' she replies, pretending this is an acceptable response in an appointment with a psychiatrist you have been referred to because everyone could tell that you weren't very well at all.

The woman smiles, her eyes seeing Coral clearly. 'I'm Doctor Elkayam, by the way.' She smiles again. 'You can call me Monica.'

Coral breathes in and out slowly through her nose, and lets herself deflate slightly. She stops herself from saying that she is Coral, in return, because Monica already knows that.

'Remind me how many weeks along you are?' Monica moves her eyes from Coral's face to Coral's stomach, where the baby is now undeniably living.

'Twenty-seven,' Coral replies automatically.

'Ah, yes. So, the size of a papaya—or a bunny rabbit?' Monica replies, smiling with one corner of her brown mouth.

'Yes!' Coral replies. The app on her phone told her this week that the baby was the size of a papaya or a bunny or a chocolate cake. Coral doesn't know the normal size of any of these things, though she liked imagining a soft bunny with big hind legs curled up in there, and she had tried to find some papaya at the supermarket after work but they didn't have any. Sweet things seem to be giving her heartburn, which is difficult, because sugar is comforting. She wants to be able to eat some chocolate cake, though in secret, in case it could be construed as cannibalism.

'How is that for you?'

'It's weird.'

'Weird is a good way of describing it.'

Coral wants to know whether Monica has been pregnant before, so she asks her if she has any children, trying to show by the way she asks it that she won't mind if that information is private. Coral doesn't like to impose on people, or to be told she shouldn't have done what she has done. It feels almost unbearable to be told you have stepped over an invisible line.

'Yes, I have two children. They are grown up—which makes me very old. They take care of me now, I suppose you could say.'

Coral is glad that Monica is kind. She can tell she is kind, and that she is perceptive, and it's a relief. Coral has been treated by doctors in the past who have seemed to be in the wrong profession, and who knew everything without having to ask, without having to care.

They talk a little about Monica's children (Paul and Elise, the law and the climate, beautiful and handsome, if I do say so myself) before Monica guides the conversation back to Coral, and the chocolate papaya bunny.

'My referral from your social worker says you've been feeling a bit disconnected from the pregnancy. Does that sound like the correct assessment?'

Something has clicked over since Coral saw the unfriendly midwife and spoke to the friendly social worker on the phone, both of whom were quite obviously assessing whether she had any attachment to her unborn baby and both of whom decided that she didn't. They had been right, in a way, though it wasn't as simple or as complicated as that. Coral hadn't known the baby, and now she was starting to. She felt angry that they had wanted to force a recognition, but the anger was floppy and she couldn't grab a hold of it.

'I guess I wasn't connected, yeah. But I am now, I think.'

It is powerful to say this. Her right hand and then her left go to her belly before she realises she has moved them there with her brain. This keeps happening, both in and out of her control, and she knows it is her way of protecting this tenuous bond they now share—her and the baby. It makes her feel motherly, and it makes her feel worthy, of the hospital's time, of the baby's time, of her own time: here, now.

'And how is it for you? That connection?'

How is it? Coral asks herself, echoing Monica in her head. She feels comfortable enough to answer this question in the way that feels easiest.

'It feels...close. Like the baby is really close. Like I'm the baby's mum. Though it's hard to say it out loud.' She moves one hand up in front of her mouth now, the other one still next to the baby.

'You certainly are your baby's mum,' Monica tells her, and writes something down in her notebook.

Coral doesn't worry what she is writing—once she feels safe with someone, she finds she doesn't mind about anything else for a while.

'Close sounds nice?' Monica says.

'Yeah, it's the nice kind of close.'

Monica nods, and doesn't say anything back, and Coral knows this is because she wants Coral to be able to say more, go deeper, if she needs to. Coral wants to fill the silence up with something, even if it's not worth saying. Yet it seems like Monica can tolerate silence well. It helps Coral feels as though she could, too. They sit together for a few seconds longer.

'I can't imagine it, though,' Coral says. She really can't. She doesn't even know what a newborn baby looks like. Will she feel a rush of love when it comes out? Will she think it's beautiful even if it looks like a raisin? She hopes so.

'Motherhood?' Monica asks.

'Yes.'

'Well, no, I expect you can't.' Monica pauses to shift her glasses back up her nose with one finger, then to write in the notebook. Coral relaxes her body again—it tends to tense back up if she doesn't mind it.

'No,' Coral says.

They talk about Coral's mental-health history—her obsessive-compulsive disorder diagnosis, her treatment, the symptoms then and now. Monica asks Coral if she identifies with the diagnosis.

'Do you mean, do I agree that I have it?'

'Yes. Exactly. Does it sit right inside you? Do you see your symptoms and recovery the way those who've treated you see them?'

Coral hasn't thought about this before, not really. She supposes that's because she is lucky. She does agree that she has OCD, or she had it and she still has it sometimes, or she will always have it. She's never felt ashamed of the illness, and she's not sure exactly why, because she knows it is stigmatised. Perhaps it's because Topaz has always held her head high, and encouraged Coral to hold hers high too, even when she's being critical. Or because Coral truly doesn't believe that mental illness is something to be ashamed of. She tells people if they need to know, and doesn't if they don't. If they see her tics, she brushes it off internally—the tics are a symptom, they don't define her. Maybe she is in denial about her shame, but it doesn't feel like it.

She tells Monica this, and Monica writes it down.

The session is not like any other session Coral has had with a psychiatrist. Monica seems to want to understand her personal and emotional experience, and gives her a whole hour. At the end, she tells Coral what she is thinking and asks for Coral's feedback. It is as if Coral is in charge, and Coral has never been in charge before.

'I think the dosage you are taking at the moment is working for you,' Monica says. 'Would you agree?'

Coral would, in this moment, while everything feels okay, and says so.

'And it's as safe for the baby as we can get it, so we will leave you on that dose for now, okay?'

Coral nods. She is happy to keep taking her medication. It helps her not to spiral up or down into paralysing panic, or fear.

'What have your intrusive thoughts been like?'

Coral had forgotten that she might be asked this. Monica is a psychiatrist, and she knows that someone with OCD will always experience some symptoms, despite their treatment plans: their medication and psychological coaching and healthy lifestyle and knowledge-equals-power. She doesn't want to tell Monica about the occasional intrusive thought she's been having of killing the baby. It gives the wrong impression—as if she wants to do it—and takes things on an unpleasant trajectory. She is sure she's okay. The thoughts aren't as real as they could be, and they're not constant. She tells herself it makes more sense not to share them.

'Haven't been having many. No more than usual. Maybe once a week I'll have one when I'm walking near traffic, or when I have lots to do and feel more anxious.'

This sounds normal, and Monica nods to confirm that it is. She writes something else down in her notebook, but it's barely anything. She doesn't ask Coral how her tics have been—the tapping, the checking, the shrugs. Coral doesn't tell her the tapping has been worse, that the shrugging is coming back. Instead she discreetly taps the side of her chair, and smiles and nods and smiles again.

'I'd like you to try some formalised meditation each day, perhaps around twenty minutes of sitting and focusing on your breath. The nostrils are a good place, as they're neutral. Does that sound doable?'

Coral tells Monica that it does. She is excited to have a reason to sit and look after herself. To establish a routine, and commune with peace, the way healthy people do.

'If you find that you start having scary or overwhelming thoughts when you try to do this, stop, and let me know. Okay?'

Coral nods, and crosses her fingers that she won't.

✧

After agreeing again to the plan of daily meditation, and agreeing to a plan to see Dr Elkayam again in four weeks (pineapple, bunch of asparagus), Coral feels lighter in her body than she has since the baby has been in there, sprouting.

She shakes herself out and drums her lips together, to make sure she is rid of any worry from not telling Monica the entire truth, and hops down the steps outside the hospital, putting her headphones on when she reaches the bottom, to listen to Jen Cloher and Solange on her walk home. It will take her forty minutes to get from the sliding doors of the hospital to her front door, with its flywire front and its peephole and its peeling painted wood. She wants to feel some emotions on the way.

7

IN THE THIRTIETH week, on the Saturday, it is Coral's thirtieth birthday, and the omens flock, like owlet-nightjars after dusk in the botanical gardens.

She meets Amber for breakfast at their usual place in the morning, and Amber is there before her, poised like a swan on a lake. Coral sits down, making sure not to hit her round belly on the edge of the table as she does, and they smile at each other. Amber is wearing her Baltic amber necklace: the deep flame orange of the stone is arresting against her pale pink skin. She reaches for her bag and rustles around inside it, then brings out a small wrapped object.

'For you. Happy birthday,' she says, and hands Coral the little something. It isn't particularly heavy, but it does have some weight to it.

Coral has had an unsettled night, moving around her

crumpled bed, trying to get comfortable, and she has been awake and up since before dawn. She is quivering with fatigue, and notices herself tapping the side of her chair with her right fingers. She wishes it wasn't her birthday, but it is, and she does appreciate the care.

'Aw—thank you! Should I open it?' she asks.

'Yes!' says Amber, smiling as much as she ever does.

Coral peels each bit of sticky tape off, managing not to rip the threaded silver wrapping paper, and underneath it is a little black box with a snug lid. She supposes it is jewellery—something impeccably elegant, that she will never be able to wear without imagining Amber wearing it better. She doesn't think Amber is deliberately more poised than everyone else, but she knows that Amber knows she is.

Before she has a chance to open up the box, a waiter comes to take their order. Coral is hungry, but she can't fit much in. Amber orders her waffles, and Coral asks the man who is serving them what kind of sweets they have.

'Today we have cardamom croissants, and orange cannoli, and freshly baked rock cakes.'

Rock cakes. Coral isn't sure she knows what a rock cake is, but everything at this cafe is always delicious, and she likes the idea of pretending she is eating something dug up from the earth (a vegetable, some quartz). The waiter nods when she says she will have one, and Amber looks amused.

'A rock cake,' she says. 'I remember trying to eat one of those when I was little, and giving up.'

Coral seems to have a faint memory of something like this, too, but she is sure the cafe wouldn't serve the kind of rock cakes that even little children couldn't demolish.

She nods her head at the box, and Amber nods her head to say yes, open it. Inside is some black tissue paper, wrapped around something small. She lifts it out and carefully pulls the tissue paper back. It is a polished piece of orange stone, in the shape of an oval. The stone has some red flecks in it (desert dirt or blood). She supposes it is a piece of amber, like her seahorse, but that maybe this one really does have special powers.

'Is it amber?' she asks Amber.

'Yes,' Amber replies, smiling. 'It's another from my babcia's collection. It reminded me of you, for some reason, when I saw it.' Amber says this sincerely, and Coral's heart glows orange in her chest.

'Thank you, Amb. It's so beautiful.'

The stone is gleamy and smooth and cold to touch. Coral holds it up to her cheek and presses it against her soft skin. It feels nice there. Amber raises her eyebrows and purses her lips, as if she has been pushed past her sentimentality, her magic, her intuitive communication threshold for the day. Coral moves the stone away and her cheek feels bereft.

'It's not for wearing, just for holding,' Amber tells her, and this sounds right. Coral will keep it next to her bed, on the bedside table she fashioned out of a few bits of plywood and some bricks years ago. She should get a proper bedside table, now that she's having a baby.

Coral puts the beautiful stone in her pocket and it glows in there, cool and serene, while she attacks her rock cake, and Amber devours her waffle stack. The rock cake looks like a little jagged mountain that a goat might climb, and tastes sweet and pleasantly fruity. It crumbles as she prods it with her fork, so she picks up the little bits of erosion with her fingers, and places them carefully on her tongue. Amber doesn't want to try the rock cake, but Coral does try Amber's waffles—for the first time, despite all those orders over many weekends. They are just like waffles should be, with too much syrup.

'I spoke to Beata and Jurek yesterday,' Amber tells her, after she has finished her meal, and is holding her cup of tea with both hands. 'They send you their love.'

Beata and Jurek. Coral hopes she will see them again one day. It feels so long ago that she sat in their kitchen in Bobolin and was fed by them, and Beata guessed that she was pregnant, and Gosia died. She still can't imagine them actually living in that small, empty place, and wonders how long they will last, now that Gosia is gone. She imagines a pet for them, and a baby, but perhaps they are past that stage of possibility—perhaps they live for each other, or something greater, like the world.

'It must be getting warmer there now?' Coral says, after she realises that it must be, and remembers that Bobolin comes alive in the summer, with all the holidaymakers who have been hibernating across Europe through the cold. Amber nods.

'It'd be nice to see Bobolin in summer,' Coral adds. She can't imagine it, not really. It will always be grey and cold in her memories, and she can't replace that grey and cold with warmth and sun and shadows.

'I don't think I'll ever go back there,' Amber says, and she doesn't seem to mind.

Coral admires Amber's ability to see things clearly. She herself feels tied to Bobolin, after their trip there and the passing of Gosia, but Amber knows that it is just a place, and the world is big, and she won't live forever. Pain vibrates through Coral at that—she won't live forever, but she is bringing a baby into the world. She feels the burn of her heart in her chest. Too much rock cake, not enough water. Then the waiter is there with a full carafe, and he places it just in front of Coral's plate.

'Thank you,' she says.

After they leave the cafe, they walk together to the tram stop, where Coral will catch a tram to lunch with Ruby, and from there to see Topaz for afternoon tea. It is a full day, and she reminds herself to be grateful. The heartburn is distracting her head—it seems to do that thoroughly—but she hugs Amber and thanks her again for the stone, taking it out of her pocket so they can both admire it again.

'Don't lose it,' Amber says. 'Make sure you put it somewhere safe,' she adds, and then she is gone.

Coral waits for a tram, and tries not to shriek or spit on the ground. She needs to do something quickly, though, before she disappears. She loves Amber and Amber loves her, but her oldest friend's ways make Coral wild sometimes. There's an empty chip packet lying on the ground near her feet. She bends down with effort, picks it up and scrunches it, before throwing it down again—her very existence a rebellion.

After she is seated, and a few stops have come and gone, the tram stops suddenly on the corner of Brunswick Street and Victoria Parade. The lurch smacks Coral forward into the seat she is facing, her belly banging against the fabric of it. She is stuck there for a few seconds, panting, and then she pulls herself back and sits down, her hands on her stomach and her heart beating, so fast, in her neck. She didn't hit the seat hard, and she is sure the baby is okay, but her body is terrified, and the tram doesn't seem to be moving, is stuck in between two stops, snaking the corner of the roads. No one is near her on the tram; no one has seen her, a pregnant woman, hurt herself, right where the baby is growing. She wishes someone had, so they could help her. Tears come up from her chest into her eyes and down her cheeks. The heartburn worsens. She stands to ask the tram driver what is wrong, why they have stopped here. She hopes they will see that she is pregnant and be gentle with her.

The driver is a woman, and she doesn't seem to be able to hear Coral, though there is only a screen full of holes between them.

'Excuse me,' Coral says for the third time, loudly, but the driver doesn't flinch, and just keeps pulling at levers and muttering under her breath, as if she is all alone and the machine she is driving has stopped, which it has.

'Can you hear me?' Coral asks, trying one last time. The driver does not falter, her ears do not prick, and Coral gives out a large sigh that is also not heard, or is ignored. She moves away from the window to try to see if she can get off the tram, or ask another passenger what they think might be happening.

There doesn't seem to be anyone on the tram anymore, though Coral is sure there were other passengers when she got on, and that they didn't all alight at the few stops she sat through. She could feel the energy of them, and when the tram stopped suddenly, she was sure she had heard a gasp or two, down the other end of the two carriages that are joined together with a bendy bit like an accordion. She rubs her eyes, partly because they are smarting, and partly because she is hoping they will clear her vision and she won't be alone anymore, but when she takes her fists away there is still no one on the tram but her.

She pulls the cable that signals she would like to get off at the next stop and hears its buzz, then she presses one of the buttons that does the same, and sees the little globe up above the driver's box lit up, but the doors don't open, of course—they are in between stops.

'Please let me out,' she shouts, loud and clear, to the driver. Nothing happens.

She puts her hand in her pocket and touches the cool amber stone. The doors creak open. There's no time to work out whether the driver has finally heard her or the doors have just opened of their own accord (was the amber listening?). She needs to get out before they close again, so she heaves herself gently down the steps of the nearest exit, and onto the bitumen of Victoria Parade, where the cars are slowly moving around either side of the tram, as if it is a beached whale.

She hopes someone will ask her if she is okay, so she can interact and pop through the bubble that seems to surround her. She can see people—in their cars, walking on the street, waiting at the tram stop—but none of them are looking at her, even though she is visibly with child, and has just alighted a tram that has stopped in the wrong place (a dying pilot whale on the sand). She feels like screaming out, so they will notice her—isn't society supposed to look after mothers? She has never felt looked after, and now she is expected to look after something else, without help.

She is close to a hospital, the one that stands tall and stately at the edge of the Carlton Gardens, all red brick and important signs. If she goes in and tells them she has been in a tram accident, they will have to make sure she is okay, that the baby is okay. Maybe she can tell them it's her birthday too. She would like someone to be very kind to her, if possible.

She sends Ruby a text message after dodging cars and crossing the road: *Hey lovely. The tram I was on stopped and I hit my tummy. Not badly. I'm going to go into St Vincent's and see if everything is okay with baby. Can we meet afterwards? X*

It's almost a hot day, even though it's August, late winter, and should be cool and brisk. The sun beats down on Coral's head, telling her to get inside. Her phone buzzes as she walks towards the doors of the emergency department, holding her stomach, which is still aching a bit, though she can't tell if that's just because her brain knows it should be aching, it could be aching, rather than because it actually is. Her phone buzzes: *Darling!! Oh my gosh! So glad you can see them now and make sure! ♡♡♡ Just let me know when and where!! ♡♡♡*

Ruby always has the most exclamation marks and love hearts in her messages, and at the end of every sentence she says in real life. She lives in East Melbourne, in an old posh apartment complex overlooking pristine public gardens that nobody seems to use. They were planning to throw a rug out in these gardens and share a birthday picnic lunch—Ruby isn't working today, at the florist where she sells canna lilies to elegant women with white hair. She will have bought lots of yummy things for them to eat, and Coral hopes that the baby and her stomach are fine, so she can go and enjoy it all soon. She can feel the piece of Baltic amber glowing cool in her pocket as she enters—through one of the side doors, as she can't seem to get the automatic doors to open for her. It is as though the stone is the same temperature as the Baltic Sea.

At the triage counter, Coral stops and stands where she thinks is the right place, at the arrow on the floor pointing towards the window. There is no one else waiting, which seems unusual. Coral watches the nurses behind the perspex, and the one who seems to be first triage nurse looks up as if to see her, then looks back down.

Coral waits, and watches the nurse take slow sips of something from a mug, scratch her head, talk to the other nurses, laugh, stand up and stretch, look at the watch on her wrist, yawn, and sit back down again. The nurse is ignoring her.

Coral moves forward, her legs angry, her arms angry. She is clearly pregnant, and even if she wasn't, this is a triage desk. The nurse needs to acknowledge her and listen to her, and instead she is acting as if Coral doesn't exist. At the counter, she clears her throat and speaks into the perforated section of the perspex, where her voice can travel through to the nurse's ears.

'Excuse me? I've been waiting for a while. Can I please talk to someone? I'm pregnant, and I fell and hit my stomach.'

Coral can hear that her voice is faltering, because the nurse has not looked up, and does not seem to have heard her, though she must have. There is a small red rage (a squiggle) in her head. She is pregnant. What is wrong with this woman? Why does everyone act as if she is not important?

'Excuse me!' she yells. 'Hey!'

The nurse busies herself with some papers, then picks up a pile and says to one of the other nurses sitting in the perspex box that she is going to give the files to a doctor, and asks that they cover her.

Tears sprout in Coral's eyes, and she is suddenly finding it difficult to breathe. It's as if all the things she might have been angry or sad about in her life, since her pregnancy, about anything and everything, have come up at once, and she is gasping, and overheated, and overwhelmed.

'Please,' she says, with water in her voice, but none of the nurses betray having heard her at all. Her stomach has been resting against the counter edge, and she pulls it back and turns. She will not wait any longer. No one can help her, and she is utterly alone.

Coral texts Ruby and tells her that she is okay but she needs to rest, then waits for a tram to take her back down Brunswick Street so she can go home and crawl into her soft bed to cry. The weather is still warm, and she wishes she was just her, without this thing growing on the inside that is making everything harder, and more scary. She wants to be a different version of herself, and to drink down a big glass of something strong and float away. Instead, she watches the people outside the tram as it crawls, biting her tongue to keep the rest of the tears inside until she is home.

⟡

After the crying in the bed, the days keep going—on and on. It has been a particularly mild August, but Coral can't seem to feel glad about it, though she has always enjoyed warmer weather. It's hard being pregnant in the sun, she has discovered. She has always assumed that it would be but the particulars never needed to be made clear. Now, her body tells her—extreme thigh rub, extreme breast sweat, swollen feet so her shoes won't fit, a hot body getting even hotter, with no relief.

She has been trying to do the mindfulness meditation each day, prescribed by Dr Monica, but she is finding it difficult to keep still, and her thoughts seem to scream when she tries to move away from them and focus on the breath at her nostrils. It's as if the thoughts are always there, mumbling about how easy it would be for her to kill her baby, or for her to kill herself or someone else, if she wanted to; when she sits and is quiet and listens to them, they are so excited, they won't let her go. Coral is used to having graphic, insistent thoughts. They have been popping into her head since she was a child, and she knows how to put up boundaries for them, with the help of medication. She wonders, though, if the pregnancy has somehow shifted back the power to their side.

Three separate people tell her, 'You must be so excited,' in a matter of days, and Coral doesn't tell any of them what she thinks when they say that, because they would be astonished to learn that no, she is not so excited, and actually she is terrified, and irritated by everything, including them.

She has another appointment with Dr Monica, in which she is too tired to say much about anything (screaming thoughts, terrible fears), and in which Monica seems to be satisfied that things are going along as well as they can be for someone with a chronic mental illness who is having a baby on her own. She doesn't tell Dr Monica that the meditation is hard, though she said she would. She doesn't hear from the social worker or the midwives, and the bang on her belly from the tram doesn't give her any more pain, so she decides to forget about it.

Coral is reading a book of Anne Sexton's poetry. Each poem is a grim fairytale, mostly about how difficult it is to be a mother, when you don't want to be consumed by something but you are expected to be and you can't help but be, and you are also not as much as you should be, as well as too much. She has read the Hansel and Gretel poem over and over, and finds she likes to read it before bed, even though it could very easily make her feel anxious and worried about motherhood. Coral often finds that she gains comfort from things that might be seen as dreadful and unnerving to others. To hold a little bit of the darkness of the world makes her feel as if she could handle more.

She wouldn't tell anyone this, except for Ruby, perhaps, who would likely find it funny, and guffaw at it with her big, white mouth, but Coral gets hungry sometimes when she reads this poem, after the line describing the author's child as 'my chicken biddy' as 'sweet as fudge', with a 'neck as smooth as a hard-boiled egg'. She knows this is supposed to be taboo, but she understands what Anne Sexton meant.

The only part that scares her is the last section, when the mother suggests to the father that they deliberately 'lose the children in the forest', to be rid of them and have all the bread to themselves. It scares her because she can imagine herself to be the mother who plans to lose her child. Not because she will want the bread all to herself, but because she might not want the bread (or the baby).

8

CORAL MEETS TOPAZ for their Sunday-night meal at the Italian place, and she realises as she waits there, for Topaz who is late, that something has loosened inside her. It has loosened its hold on Topaz, and how frustrating she can be, and how difficult Coral has always found that, and how she has always tried to deny this because it is painful to dislike your own mother. The loosening has happened without her realising, and it seems to mean that Topaz's actions are not needling her the way they usually would. She treads lightly around this phenomenon, and tries to be very grateful for it. Coral knows that freedom like this rarely lasts.

After Coral has finished the cherry mocktail she ordered when she arrived, Topaz saunters in as if she is right on time, and Coral doesn't even feel a twinge in her chest—in fact, she is amused by her mother's insouciance. The drink was sweet and tangy, and Coral feels heavy and round and plush, so she lets her mother bend down for a kiss instead of standing.

'I've had a long day,' Topaz tells her, after ordering 'just a glass of something red with body' when the same meek waitress who seems to work every Sunday evening asked what she would like to drink. She is unwrapping a silk scarf that has been circled around her neck and it is so long that she is still doing it by the time her wine arrives. The silk has a pattern that looks like it could be leaves or wings. Coral reflects on how leaves and wings look similar.

'It's hot at the moment, as you know,' Topaz tells her, 'and I was supposed to be meeting a friend for lunch in the park but neither of us could bear the idea of the sun, so we decided to go and see the new exhibition at the Ian Potter instead.'

Topaz has a vast array of eccentric friends. They do leisurely, decadent things together, like cheese platters and a film, or rowing on a lake, or museums and sparkling wine on promenades. Coral didn't get Topaz's fondness for the finer things in life. She is quite happy with a cask of dry white and a ratty-blanket picnic.

She nods. She doesn't need to say much when Topaz is telling her a story. Nods are enough, because her mother always assumes that she is engaged, and listening intently.

'Well. That was a bad idea!' Topaz says, laughing lightly at the end. 'The Ian Potter was full of schoolchildren, you see.'

Coral sees. Topaz can't abide children. She hadn't liked Coral as a school-aged girl, and had told her, explaining that it was simply because of her age, that they would be friends when she was older. Coral assumes it is because children aren't yet polite enough to pretend they are hanging on her every word, and might not be able to follow her grand stories with anything like interest.

'So we went to Sharon's house, which is near the Ian Potter, you see, and she made us a salad and had some bread, so we were able to eat there, with coffee and amaretto afterwards,' Topaz explains, and Coral once again wonders at the amount of detail her mother seems to think people want: about her every moment, and everything she ate and drank and thought about. Perhaps Topaz being such a chatterbox is why Coral doesn't bother talking all that much. There doesn't seem to be any point—it has all already been said.

She is half-listening and twirling the cold empty glass around on the tablecloth with her fingers when she hears the word 'amber'.

'And so I asked if I could keep it, and she said I could. I wanted to show you.'

Topaz seems to be taking something out of her pocket, and then it's clear that she has indeed taken something out of her pocket and is holding it out towards Coral, who opens up her hand and receives, as if she is a puppet, on strings.

It's a small piece of smooth amber, just like the piece Amber gave Coral for her birthday, from Gosia's collection. It feels cool and solid, like the other piece does, and it hums on her palm.

Topaz is smiling at her, expectantly. She knows Coral likes gemstones, and that she will like this one. The orange is lighter than Gosia's Baltic stones, and Coral wonders where this amber comes from.

'Amber is the stone of courage,' Topaz tells her.

Coral knows this, was told this or read this somewhere at some point. It feels right that a cool orange stone would be the stone that emboldens the heart.

'For the birth, I give you this courage,' Topaz says, smiling. 'And for the years ahead,' she adds, with a laugh.

Coral is touched, and she curls her fingers around the little piece of amber, so precious and soothing, and smiles back. She won't laugh: she doesn't have it in her today to echo someone else to that extent. But she can smile, and appreciate Topaz's sentiment. Where there might have been a wave of pissed-off crashing inside her because Topaz seems to think Coral needs help to be courageous, there is only calm water. She taps her thigh, then rubs her belly, to thank the baby.

'You're looking very large,' Topaz says, her blue eyes on Coral's rounded front.

'Yes, Mum. I'm having a baby.'

'Very funny. I meant you look larger than when I last saw you. It's a good thing, you know. Means that baby of yours is growing well, will be healthy, chubby.'

Coral hopes so. She wants nothing but splendid thriving for the baby.

'You were a fat little thing when you came out,' Topaz adds, because she has to, it seems.

'Yes, you've told me,' Coral says, but she doesn't mind. A fat baby is a healthy baby. They have already drummed that into her at the hospital. She takes a big breath into her diaphragm, which is somewhere there, beneath the fleshy mound.

'I fed you with my breasts for a whole year,' Topaz says, and looks down at her front with a laugh.

Topaz is flat-chested, and Coral can't imagine how her breasts could have fed anyone, but of course they would have swelled somewhat, with the milk. Topaz has passed down her small, triangular breasts to Coral, though at the moment they are full and round from the pregnancy. In the mirror when she sees them she is taken aback—even her nipples are fuller.

They order their meals, and the meals come and they eat them, with some companionable silence, the type that comes when you lived together for many years (and shared a body). Coral's lasagne is silky and tart—the cheese is almost on the turn, the way she likes it. Topaz stabs at the olives in her chicken cacciatore, gets red sauce on her chin like all mothers do, and slurps her wine, managing to remain charming all the while. She tells Coral about what it was like when Coral had just been born and they were living in the terrace in Carlton with the flatmates, and everyone helped to look after her, and there was a leak in the bathroom and in the kitchen, and one of the flatmates bravely climbed up on the roof to put buckets on the holes, like hats.

'They all loved you,' Topaz tells her, again. 'Heaven knows why!'

Coral is again glad for those straggly thirty-somethings who helped her mother raise her. Maybe she can introduce the baby to them: another generation, healthy and new.

✧

On the street, Coral asks Topaz if she knows where the amber stone is from.

'What do you mean?' her mother asks.

'Don't worry,' Coral says.

They hug, and she smells Topaz's familiar skin.

'I won't,' her mother says.

9

THIRTY-FIVE WEEKS, THEN thirty-six. The baby is a hairy coconut, then a romaine lettuce (cos). Coral finishes up at work, and says goodbye to her colleagues, gladly, because she is so exhausted that she has a dark half-moon under each eye. Roy gives her a long hug that feels like a cocoon, and kisses her cheek with his dry lips, telling her what it would be like to have them on hers, and helping her to be gladder it never happened. Steve gives her a present, 'chosen by the girls', and when she opens it and sees a tiny playsuit with pretty blue hearts all over she starts to cry because the baby will wear this, and while it is wearing this, she will love it and it will need her.

She is glad to let go of the pressure of the news, and the hours in front of her computer trying to word things in a way that will entice the most readers while also staying true to the story, the facts. She doesn't know if she will ever go back to it, though Steve says she can, if she wants, once the baby is a child.

She doesn't go to the antenatal classes that the hospital recommends, and she doesn't know why. She is enrolled, but the weekend of the first class arrives and she doesn't get ready or leave the flat, and she misses her chance. She doesn't tell anyone, and no one calls her to ask where she is or, later, to ask why she didn't go. It strikes her, again, that she shouldn't be having this baby.

She is so large now, around her middle, that she can't pull her chair very far in at tables, or move through narrow spaces. She stops leaving the house much, because she doesn't have to. When she does leave, women on the street tell her she is having a boy—that her belly is sitting high and this is how they know. She doesn't know whether she would like a boy or a girl. Her wish that it be a girl has faded.

She meets Jasper again in the thirty-seventh week, when the baby is a honeydew melon. She has never liked eating melons, their flavours too mild and watery, too apologetically sweet. She supposes this is a good thing, if she has one growing inside her. Jasper suggests they meet for lunch at the Vic Market on a Saturday, and Coral imagines how overwhelming it will be, with all the people and her belly hanging off her like a growth, a vulnerability. Then she imagines ordering a sausage with sauerkraut from the bratwurst stall, and her mouth waters.

Jasper looks almost handsome, standing with his hands in his pockets on the corner of Elizabeth and the street with the McDonald's, on the corner where the buskers play. He is wearing a navy shirt that might be corduroy or linen, and she shivers as she approaches him, imagining taking it off him later, him leaning down to lick her tummy, his fingers quickly entering her. She doesn't think about sex much at the moment, but when she does, it's a whole mouthful. She can taste it, and wants to hear herself moan and command. If she is home when this happens she tries to masturbate, but it is difficult to reach the hood of her clitoris without stretching, and the need for navigation takes away the drive. She ordered a vibrator online a few weeks ago and has been using it instead—has had some orgasms so crashing and shaky (wham!) that she quickly had to take the thing out and lie back on the bed, panting, so it didn't burst her whole body open.

He doesn't see her until she is nearly upon him, his eyes resting on something up and to the side, perhaps at the architecture, perhaps at nothing. When his eyes meet hers they are shy, and he smiles gingerly. 'How are you?'

'Very pregnant,' she answers, and laughs, because of course she is, and that doesn't answer the question. 'How are you?'

'I'm good,' he says, though he isn't: she can tell.

They walk into the old building that houses the market's delicatessens and each order a sausage—she a sweaty beef and cheese with sauerkraut and mustard, he a spicy pork with tomato sauce. The food takes a while, and as they stand waiting, not knowing what to say, Jasper takes her hand very briefly and rubs her palm with his rough thumb. It feels comforting, and when Coral looks at his face after he has let go, she appreciates the faint lines at either side of his eyes. They mean he is ageing, and he is real, and maybe she can know him.

'Sorry,' he says, from the side of his mouth. 'I wanted to touch you.'

They have sex in the hallway of her place, where she takes him after the sausages, and she can taste the pork on his tongue. He brings a stool from her kitchen, sits her up on it and tilts her backwards so he can push inside her, telling her at the same time how sexy she is. She lets herself lean back into these words, though she doesn't feel sexy—she feels like a balloon that is about to pop at a children's birthday party, ruining the innocence. Afterwards, she brings him to her couch and they lie there together, him circled like a king prawn around her belly, his hot pork breath on her ear.

She wonders if they'll keep fucking every so often and that'll be it, or if they will fall in love, though she can't imagine that. Coral feels like she won't have much choice either way, like everything is happening to her, lately, and maybe forever, not because of her or in spite of her. She doesn't mind; it's easier this way. Jasper seems to be wondering the same thing, about the fucking or the love, as he strokes her hair awkwardly and tells her things.

He wiggles himself down, kissing her clavicle with oily lips. 'I think about you a lot,' he says, to her neck.

She doesn't really think of him all that much, but it wouldn't make sense if she told him this. She doesn't want to cause him pain, and she wouldn't know how to explain that she doesn't think of him because there's no room to.

'That's nice,' she replies, and nestles her nose into his hair, because she likes his hair. She hopes liking his hair is enough.

10

THE BABY COMES slightly early, at the start of October. At thirty-nine weeks, when it is fully cooked but not yet due, it emerges from Coral's vagina like a sea urchin from a shell, though with much more blood and gratuitous violence.

They tell her the baby is a boy and he is healthy, but before that, she suffers.

⟡

Coral has Braxton Hicks contractions all the way through her thirty-eighth week. She knows they are not real because the midwives tell her so, when she arrives three days in a row at the hospital expecting to give birth.

At the beginning of her thirty-ninth week the Braxton Hicks stop, and a day later Coral's waters break. She is at home, in bed, in the mid-morning, trying to read poetry but getting distracted by the burn across her chest from the bowl of chopped-up peaches she tried to eat for breakfast, when she feels a wetness under her. Lifting up the doona, she sees a big soggy circle below her big wet body. She is shocked, for a second—takes a sharp inward breath and doesn't let it out for a while—but then feels eerily calm. She changes her undies, calls an ambulance and her mother, and sends a text to Ruby, her birth partner, who will hold her hand. *My waters broke. See you at the hospital x*

After a woozy moment of trying to think, she copies the text and sends it to Amber, then to Jasper. She wants them to be there, waiting outside, so they can come in and meet the baby, afterwards.

The paramedics are kind and tall, and they help Coral to the ambulance with gentle encouragement. She is waddling, and leaning forward from the pain, and her breasts seem to be leaking. As soon as the waters broke and the bed was soaked, the real contractions started, and they are sweeping through her like flames through a forest, before she has a chance to brace herself. The contractions seem close together but the paramedics tell her the gap is more than five minutes, and this means there is time. When a contraction comes, starting at her back and ending in her pelvis, Coral's mind flicks between clawing the baby out with her bare hands and the baby dying inside her from the pain they are enduring together.

'Do the contractions hurt the baby?' she asks the taller of the two tall paramedics.

He smiles, and puts his handsome hand on her shoulder. 'Nah, sweetheart. The baby's the one making the contractions.

It's ready to come out.'

She imagines the baby banging on her insides, demanding escape. She doesn't know how she will cope with such insolence when it's on the outside.

'You got someone meeting you at the hospital?' the slightly less tall paramedic shouts back at her from the driver's seat.

'Yes,' she answers, breathlessly, at the end of a twisted cramping agony, and thank goodness. The pain feels like it has ruined her already; she doesn't know how she is going to last if this goes on too long. Ruby will soothe her with her honey voice and silkiness, her belief that everything is always okay.

The paramedics help her get to the maternity triage desk, and there she is told she will be assessed to see whether she is in active labour by a pretty midwife with cold hands, who takes her wrist pulse before they move to a small room with a bed on wheels.

Coral takes off her pants and her underwear and lies down, with difficulty, because she is in the middle of the pain again, and she can't help panting a bit and groaning, and the midwife gently asks her to widen her legs so she can feel how far off baby might be. She tells her that she will put her fingers inside to see how open Coral's cervix is.

Coral spreads her legs as wide as she can—she wants to know exactly what to expect, even though she knows this isn't possible—and the midwife makes a few small noises as she inserts two gloved fingers and moves around inside. Soon Coral is sitting up on the bed with her undies and her pants back on, being told by the pretty midwife that she is ready to go to the birth suite, because the baby is coming.

Terror (the beginning of another contraction?) rocks Coral's core, and a picture of herself lying in a bed on wheels surrounded by blood flashes through her mind, then a picture of the pretty midwife holding a dead baby, her baby, dead. She clenches her teeth to get rid of the pictures, and it works—her mind is clear.

She asks the midwife to tell Ruby where to come when she gets here. The midwife seems to know Ruby: she nods her head and smiles and says of course, she will get Ruby straight to Coral's side as soon as she arrives. Coral clenches her teeth again—the midwife can't know Ruby, that's not possible—but the midwife is still there after she softens her jaw, and she guides Coral to the lift and takes her one level up, to a small room painted in cream and with flowers and machines in each corner. Another contraction is coming, she can feel it in her lower back: she already feels like an expert of how this pain begins and ends.

The pretty midwife says goodbye; she looks most pretty when she is frowning, as she does just before she pats Coral's hand with her cold fingers and leaves her there in the suite with other midwives whom Coral doesn't like the look of, because they are not the pretty one.

Coral hopes Ruby will be here soon; she is hot and sweaty in the small room, and none of the midwives say anything to her until another contraction comes, and she leans forward so the pain doesn't rip her open on the inside and she moans, and one of them tells her she can get up on the bed, if she likes, which she does. Lying down doesn't work with the contraction, so she sits up on the bed, bending herself forward as much as someone with a belly as big as a mountain can lean forward, and sips little bits of air in through her half-open mouth.

One of the midwives, who has orange curly hair tied back and a rosy face with taupe freckles, seems as if she has been in this room forever and knows what she is doing. She tells Coral to take off all her clothes this time, and to put on the blue hospital gown folded up on the bed in front of her, then she pulls the curtain around Coral for privacy. Coral wishes she had changed her undies—they are the ones she wears at home, when she needs to let go, and the elastic is busted around the top, so they half fall off when she is standing. Coral doesn't know what to say when she is finished and is wearing just the blue gown and her tatty undies, and so she makes a small noise, and the curtain is drawn back, and the curly midwife takes her blood pressure and lets her hold her hand when the next wave of something like hot and blood inside comes, though she doesn't seem to like it.

Ruby arrives. Her cheeks are red and she is wearing her florist uniform and her voice is like almond oil.

'Corry! You poor thing! I'm here,' she says, and holds Coral's trembling hand with both of hers, kissing it, doing everything Coral needs.

It is so uncomfortable to lie on the bed, so Coral stands and leans against the wall, then bends over until her back is curved like a cat and her forearms are on the bed. Neither of these positions feel any better. She needs to have this baby out of her, her body can't bear it any longer, and the feeling is like she wants to jump up and down to dislodge whatever is stuck, but she can't.

Topaz arrives, and tuts about. Her face is a bit blurry when Coral tries to focus on it, maybe because she keeps flitting and won't be still. Coral has no energy to do anything other than nod and sweat and let tears roll down her cheeks, and Topaz appears to respect this. She can smell Ruby's perfume near her nose, and it is spicy and soothing.

The contractions come closer together, and then it has been hours and she needs to eat something but she isn't hungry at all—she feels sickly, and her legs are cramping. The curly midwife brings her orange juice in a plastic cup and she sips it through a bendy straw, but it immediately gives her the worst heartburn she has ever felt and she drops the cup on the floor, making an orange wet circle around herself. She crawls onto the bed, and on her hands and knees she moans. It helps a little bit, as if she is a big, dying animal telling the world of her suffering.

'The baby's coming quickly,' Topaz tells her, and the midwife nods.

Her baby is coming quickly.

They check her again after she moves around the room, trying positions and groaning.

'You're almost ready to push, Coral.'

When the pushing comes, she has no choice. She has to push; her body needs to push so hard that she feels like she might push herself right out the top of it and through the ceiling. She is sitting up on the bed and Ruby is close to her, so she grabs hold of Ruby's shoulders and pulls down on them, for leverage. She hears Ruby's throaty laugh, but it isn't funny. It's terrifying. What is going to come out of her? It can't possibly be a baby.

Low-bellied screams from her throat fill the room, and the midwife says she is doing well and encourages her to lie down, so she can concentrate on what her body is telling her. It's infuriating, being told to listen to such a wild animal. Never has this happened before.

The contractions are so close together now that they become one, though the beginning and the end of each is the most painful—ripping at her insides, slicing her and punching her mercilessly. Her lower back hurts so much; her legs are wobbly; she vomits onto the floor and then into a kidney dish held by her mother, who looks smudged and worried. She can hear herself screaming and moaning, and she can feel that her mouth is open, but there is a thick layer of Vaseline across everything and her hearing is coming in and out, not enough to panic but enough to be distant.

Then there is a second midwife, with short hair and a long face. She tells Coral that panting can help with the pain, and so can huffing, and she shows Coral how, with her quiet cheeks, and Coral tries it. She pushes, then she stops pushing and feels pain, then she pushes and feels pain, stops and feels pain, wonders how much longer she can last, doesn't think she can, and then there is so much pain she vomits again, and wonders if that is poo she can feel gathering around her down there but she doesn't care, and then there is pushing, and pain, and painful pushing, and then she is so tired her eyes close and she wafts away and the pain brings her back like a gunshot, a rage in her body, in her pelvis, that needs to be sated.

As Coral lies there, out of the corner of one blurry eye she sees the creature from Poland. It is sitting on a chair in the corner of the room, and it is smiling, with its scrunched-up little face. It looks happy to see her—she hasn't seen it smile before.

Her hand grips Ruby's hand tighter and she turns to see if Ruby sees the creature too, but Ruby has her eyes closed. When Coral turns back, the creature has gone, but she knows it came to tell her something, and she thinks it might have been something good.

The head pops out after she has given up and the curly midwife and the long midwife seem to be pushing for her, because she couldn't possibly push any more herself. She feels a slurp and hears a croak and then a cry and she knows they are earthside, her baby. That they are possibly a real baby, and that they are alive, despite how her body has pummelled them.

She feels cool relief trickling down like water on the rocks near waterfalls, and she holds Topaz's hand and Ruby's hand, and she can see they are both crying. The midwives have their heads close together and they are not crying—their faces are stricken, as far as Coral can see, though she could be paranoid, she has a tendency to be paranoid, though she doesn't like to admit it. One minute she is docile, as docile as a person can be, and the next she thinks everyone knows a secret but her.

Now Topaz and Ruby are watching the midwives, and one of the midwives leaves the room, hurrying, and Coral wonders whether she should push again now—though her body isn't telling her to—to get the rest of the baby out. It can't stay trapped between her legs, just a head, forever. At least she hopes not.

The baby is crying. It doesn't sound right.

‘What’s happening?’ Topaz asks the curly midwife, who shakes her head, her lips shut tight, as if she has no way of answering.

‘What’s happening!’ Coral hears herself say, in a strangled voice.

The midwife shakes her head and keeps her eyes on the space between Coral’s gaping legs, where the baby’s head must be. ‘We’re just making sure the baby is able to come through without getting hurt.’

Coral doesn’t know what this means. Surely babies know how to do this? Wouldn’t all babies get hurt upon delivery if they needed help getting out? Her stomach rolls over on itself, as if there is a vomit wave inside her, but she doesn’t quite need to open her mouth and let it crash. Just in case, she looks to where Topaz is standing and sees that she is still holding the sick dish.

Suddenly there are other people in the room—a doctor in a white coat and people in scrubs who might be nurses. The doctor is a man, and he goes straight to Coral’s open legs and moves them apart a little more with cold, gloved hands. He doesn’t say anything and he doesn’t look at her face, but she is showing him everything. The baby isn’t crying now, though she is sure she can hear some kind of heavy, infantile breathing down there. If the baby dies, she will be devastated, she realises.

‘What can I do?’ she hears herself ask, in that strangled voice again.

None of the people in uniform seem to hear her.

⟡

After the baby is free, and it feels too late for this kind of information to be given, Coral is told by the curly midwife that its little shoulder had been caught behind her sacrum, and that was why it felt like an emergency, all of a sudden, because it was. Coral can't quite remember what a sacrum is, or exactly where it is in her body, but she can't ask any more questions—she is too tired, and she has been ignored enough.

'When this happens, the baby can't take its first outside breaths, because its lungs are being squashed, and so is the umbilical cord, so baby can't breathe through you either,' the midwife says, as she fiddles with Coral's IV, her eyes on the bendy tube.

A nurse tells her it's a boy. Coral doesn't know what this means, but it feels right, and while he is inspected she waits to hold him with what she imagines is a beatific smile on her face, so exhausted and sweaty she must be giving off scent like a bear mother after a fight with a predator.

Jasper is let in, from outside where he has clearly been waiting. He stands beside her and pats her head, telling her she has done well, smiling in a way that makes his cheeks break.

Just before she holds him, and meets his shrivelled form, an image of her baby's body all squished, turning purple, suffocating, pops into Coral's head. She opens her mouth and takes a full breath into her lungs. She doesn't want her baby ever to be squashed again, by anything.

ANGELITE
The Stone of Higher Consciousness

Dream

Hazy. I am somewhere very green. A park or a forest. A thicket. I am alone: there is no one else. Then I remember my hairy baby, crawling around on the grass at my feet.

1

CORAL CAN'T SLEEP. In the days after Flint's birth she dozed in fits and starts, grabbing pockets where she could and waking as if from the dead to comfort or feed him. Now he is three weeks old, and she stays up all night while he naps in his cot, purring like a tiny cat, occasionally mewling, occasionally screaming. Her body feels like it has been twanged. Like she is a wire fence, and she hasn't stopped vibrating from the shock yet. Flint is so small, though he is the normal size for a baby, the midwife and the maternal-child-health nurse tell her. He finds it hard to hook his little mouth onto her swollen breasts, though once there he chomps and sucks voraciously.

There is a lot to do. She needs to document these early months properly—it's why she completed her journalism training. The first two weeks were taken up with trying to get him to latch. Coral was determined to breastfeed, more determined than she has ever been, but that wasn't relevant to Flint, who didn't seem hungry enough, despite crying all the time. The nurses visited and tried to help, but Coral could see the fear in their eyes.

No one told her about the difficulties of breastfeeding. She wonders whether they might have if she had gone to some antenatal classes, but what would they have said, anyway? It's very hard and might be impossible? It's another way your body isn't yours, another way you have no control? It's failure, varying degrees of failure, so close to you that it hurts more than anything? She doesn't mind now, because he did latch, eventually, with the help of the nurses who kept turning up day after day, and now she is a good mum, a right mum, and doesn't have to be ashamed and guilty for not feeding her baby the way nature intended her to.

When she has thoughts like this she shakes her head to get rid of them, but they stay. She wants to be a nature-intended mum, it's hard not to want this, given the expectations, and she feels like she is one—up all night, preparing for her baby's life to come. She sits high at her desk, typing away on her laptop, telling whoever will eventually read this what it is like to be Flint's mother. Words like 'love' and 'hope' appear on the screen. She smiles, knowingly.

People visit most days still, bringing things with them: cooked meals in Tupperware or repurposed takeaway containers, flowers, tiny outfits for Flint, deli meats and alcohol and cheese for her, so she can consume the things she wasn't allowed for so long. She doesn't want to drink the alcohol, and this surprises her. She suspects she would have one glass and drop like a fly.

Ruby comes and holds Flint and rocks him while Coral cleans and tries to eat something; Amber comes and sits with her and asks questions; Topaz bustles in and out, as if she has a key. They all love Flint—he seems to be very loveable. He doesn't cry when they hold him, and they tell her that he cries with her because he smells her milk.

In the days after Flint was born, and Coral climbed through each day and night as if time didn't exist, Ruby brought a gift for mum and baby. She was so excited to hand it to Coral: a big heavy present wrapped in too much tissue paper. She told Coral that it was a good-luck charm. Beneath the layers, Coral found a large piece of light-blue rock, and Ruby said that it was angelite, rare and powerful. It was the stone of guardian angels, she said, and it would look after them both.

The angelite stone sits in Coral and Flint's bedroom, looming near the cot, pale blue and majestic. It bothers Coral, in a way she can't put into words, particularly when she decides at night that she will actually try to get a bit of sleep. Part of her knows this is probably just her OCD, and part of her doesn't. The angelite seems to hold an omen, and omens should not be ignored or justified. Coral tries talking to the angelite, softly, sometimes, so it knows she is friendly. It makes no difference.

She googles angelite, and learns that it was named in 1804, is a variant of anhydrite, and was found and then lost and then found again, turning up for the second time in Peru in 1987. Coral was born in 1987, and maybe she was found and lost and found again before that, in another life or another realm. There could have been anything inside her mother's tummy, but it was her, and here she is, still. Anhydrite—anhydras in Greek—

means ‘without water’. The stone is parched and so is she (water doesn’t help).

⟡

Coral breastfeeds her baby over and over, one breast and then the other, and he bites her nipples sometimes, so hard she yelps out in pain and frightens him. It can’t be helped, she thinks to herself, and he is a strong little boy. The pain stays on the bitten breasts like a stain, no matter how she balms and creams them. After she breastfeeds, sometimes Coral feels a tremendous darkness wash through her, and she sobs, momentarily, as if she is bleeding tears. It ends as quickly as it begins, and she doesn’t tell anyone. The nurse who comes to see her a few times is friendly and helpful, but there doesn’t seem to be time to tell her that breastfeeding opens Coral up like she is a wound.

Jasper visits. He holds puny Flint in his big arms and smiles down at him. The first time, Jasper cries, and then Flint cries, and Jasper says it must be because Flint has extraordinary empathy capacity for a baby, and is in tune with his dad’s emotions. Coral laughs, though the laugh seems far away, and she hears it bounce for a long time after she has stopped laughing and there is nothing to laugh at anymore.

Jasper tries to kiss her and she lets him, and they flop about on Coral’s bed until she tells him she can’t, she’s not feeling like it, which is true. He accepts this, and she is grateful, though she shouldn’t have to be. She doesn’t want to float above her own body while she is having sex, looking down and feeling dizzy from the height. Also, she is sore—her vagina needs to heal. The whole of her is raw and uncomfortably tender.

Jasper suggests he stay the night sometimes, so he can feed Flint while Coral sleeps. He comments on how tired she must be, how tired she looks, and Coral feels like scratching him (on his arm, his cheek), so he will stop talking. He doesn't know that it won't help if he stays and gets up to feed Flint because his breasts are not providing anyone with milk. She doesn't tell him that she has to feed Flint, that if she doesn't, they will both fly off into the sky like dandelion seeds. They are not stable yet, together, and the breastmilk is binding them.

2

CORAL IS STILL bleeding, though the baby was born four weeks ago, and she is still wearing nappies around the house, as she cleans and hums and schemes. She has been told by Dr Carver, whom Topaz dragged her to see, that the bleeding is normal, and if it is becoming rust-coloured it is just her insides getting rid of what they need to get rid of, in the most dramatic way they can. The blood is becoming rust-coloured, and Coral is calm—calmer than she has ever been. She has flashes of thoughts that should possibly scare her but don't: dropping the baby, dropping something on the baby, someone else dropping the baby, the baby being stabbed. She knows the baby won't die: the baby is too strong. She is trying not to think of the baby as the baby—it is Flint, her son; he is real. She is sure it is working.

Topaz visits daily, and Coral gets used to her scurrying

about, asking where Coral keeps things and pretending to tidy up. Topaz has never been tidy, and Coral sees now that it is because she picks things up and puts them down and there isn't a rhyme to it. One morning, Topaz picks up Flint and puts him down somewhere else, and the calm bursts. Coral is gripped with such a fear that she can't breathe, and has to grab him, and sit down and cough until her airways come clear, because Flint could die at any moment.

After this, she feels a rope between them—her and her baby—and it is painful in her chest, like the rope is being stretched, when they are not near each other. She wonders if this is that bond, that attachment she has been asked about, that she has heard about. The one no one seems to think she and Flint have. If this is that bond, they have it, they do. It feels dangerous and serious and conditional: as if it could snap.

The sleeplessness is catching up with Coral, but she is still awake. She holds Flint wherever she goes, around the house, sometimes to the shops or the park but only momentarily. They look at each other: he watches her with his big brown eyes, lined with delicate lashes. The angelite stone glows blue in the bedroom where she never rolls up the blinds. Flint needs the darkness, and the windows are dirty and she doesn't want to clean them; there is no time. She won't let Topaz in there, to pick things up and look at them and put them down again.

Topaz makes cups of tea that are too sweet and have too much milk or not enough or none at all. She starts to make things for Coral to eat, but Coral isn't hungry, and so Topaz puts the plates down in the kitchen and perches, nibbling at the food that sits on them.

Coral wishes her mother would leave, and for the first time since she gave birth it occurs to her that alcohol might help. There is a dusty bottle of Grenache in the pantry, so she twists it open and takes a sniff as soon as she is alone. She is not supposed to drink when she has to feed Flint, and she always has to feed him. She pours herself a large, pungent tumbler. After one sip, she puts it down and retches at the sink.

The nurse visits, and tells Coral she doesn't usually visit mums and babies at home this far along, but that they have been referred to a special program, and she will keep coming regularly, until Coral is feeling better. Coral feels fine, apart from the tugging at her chest when the nurse picks up Flint and takes him to another room, apart from the sleep, of which she can't seem to get any. She has energy—she's feeling better than she did when she was pregnant. She was a snail and now she has lost her shell and she's a slug and she can move, slick, through the night.

The nurse takes Flint to the other room and Coral wonders what they are doing in there. She hears whispers: Topaz and the nurse, conspiring. They might drop him, they might take him away, and so she rushes to hold him again.

Topaz takes her to see Dr Carver, and Topaz tells Dr Carver what Topaz thinks is wrong with Coral, while Coral sits tapping her fingers against the underside of her baby as she rocks him. Flint cries—he doesn't like it either. Dr Carver is different: she seems angry at Coral, and she tells her she needs to try some tablets that will help with her sleeping.

'Take one of these an hour before you would usually go to bed,' Dr Carver explains, handing Coral a piece of paper with typed information on it—a prescription, she supposes. 'Only one—these are very strong.'

'That should zonk her out,' says Topaz cheerfully, from the sidelines.

Flint is still crying. Coral coos to him but it doesn't help. She doesn't want to be told that he might be hungry—she knows he might be hungry, she is his mother, and he's almost always hungry, and he might be anything, really, who knows—so she pulls down her top, pops out her nipple, and moves his little upset mouth towards it. He suckles easily and gorges noisily, and she looks up to see Dr Carver smiling at her and Flint as if they are a miracle, but then her face is stern again.

'You must get some sleep, Coral.'

Topaz insists on walking Coral and Flint back to their flat, and preparing Coral something to eat when they arrive. Coral doesn't remember a mother like this—a mother who is acutely worried about her. It's the wrong time for this, she thinks. The right time would have been when I was young.

She eats a little bit of the tomato soup while Topaz is watching, so that she can be left alone. Food is slowing her down and she is not hungry, but she knows it's best to pretend this is not the case. The soup tastes like blood, and scalds her tongue (slurp, slurp).

Topaz watches her with Flint, her blue eyes now as green as malachite.

'Can I have a hold?' her mother asks, and it sounds like she is bleating, like a pathetic and helpless lamb. Coral and her baby are powerful—she feels it in her chest, in Flint's chest through hers. She doesn't want to peel him off her, but she has to play the part.

'Careful,' Coral says, as she hands her warm baby to the woman.

She observes closely until he is back in her arms again.

3

CORAL ASKS JASPER to stay with her that night, and for Topaz to leave, and she hears Topaz whispering on the phone before the front door closes behind her. She has been trying to express milk from her breasts into a bottle for Flint to feed from while she is sleeping, but it is impossible. Her nipples are sharp with pain, and only clumps and trickles of milk come out, despite all the pumping. She sends Jasper a text, and blocks out any thoughts that might come into her head afterwards, about how she is lazy, how Flint will die if he doesn't get enough breastmilk every day, and how it will be her selfishness that caused it. She doesn't think mothers who sleep are selfish—quite the opposite. The thoughts are unhelpful and unfriendly sometimes, and it is better to be quick to silence them. *Can you pls bring some baby formula? You can get it from the supermarket. I think it comes in big tins. Thanks x*

Jasper arrives, laden with formula, his face daubed with concern.

Coral is holding Flint, and she waits until Jasper has placed the big round tins on the table and then passes him their baby. Flint is bunched up and red after a crying spell—he is a tiny witch casting spells with his tears. His hands are fists and they smell like cheese, because the milk gets stuck in the creases and no matter how much you try to clean them, they get mouldy. He has cradle cap, as most babies do, and big flakes of dead skin adorn his little head with the hole in the top of it. That hole in his head terrifies Coral sometimes, and sometimes it doesn't. Flint is objectively disgusting—smelly, discoloured, rotting; face like an alien. Coral thinks he is cute, and this is how she knows she does love him.

'Hello, my boy,' Jasper is saying, holding Flint and rocking gently back and forth on his big heels.

Jasper is good with his baby, though Coral does wonder how he will go for a whole night. She feels light-headed because she hasn't eaten much, again. She isn't hungry, and the thought of eating a plate of food makes her feel like she might vomit. She watches Jasper as she stands, trying not to wilt, to faint, and he lifts Flint up and sniffs his nappy.

'Think he might need a change,' Jasper says.

'I just checked him,' Coral snaps back.

She stomps to the bedroom and throws herself on the bed. She is so sick of all these people assuming she needs them to help her, when all she needs is time and space, and peace. She expects Jasper to follow, but he doesn't, and soon she hears mumbling, then whispering, then humming. He must be changing Flint's nappy, though Flint's nappy was clean only minutes ago; she checked, she knows she did.

A flash of herself walking back into the kitchen and poking her finger through Flint's soft spot, his anterior fontanelle, his most glaring vulnerability, to show Jasper what she is capable of, visits her and then leaves. She doesn't want to do it, but sometimes the thought comes because she is tired and her breasts hurt. She reminds herself of this and strokes her own hair as if her hand is someone else's, someone who cares about her and loves her.

In the kitchen again, just one last time, Coral tells Jasper what he needs to know. 'There's soup in the fridge, made by Topaz, so it's a bit tasteless or something, but you can have some if you're hungry. There's bread in the freezer; I don't think there's butter but there's olive oil. Flint will tell you when he's hungry; you can sleep on the couch or bring the cushions to the floor. You can have my doona—I only need a blanket.'

Jasper comes over to her with Flint in his arms, as she thinks of what else she needs to say, and moves his face down towards hers. He kisses her on her forehead and she can smell him and Flint, their smells together, muddled and hot. Flint is chirping, as if he likes being close to both of them, as if he wants them to be close to him, together, all of the time.

'I'll be fine,' Jasper tells her.

✧

In bed, Coral feels as if lying down is a skill she has forgotten. She sits up, puts the sleeping tablet in her mouth and swallows it down with stale water. She squeezes an earplug into each ear, and shuffles down under the sheet and the blanket, her heart beating too fast in the left side of her chest. She can tell it is cold, but she isn't cold. If only she could laugh—that might help—but the only thing she can see near her is the poetry collection by Anne Sexton: the one where she talks of cooking up her child in the oven. She picks it up and flicks through the pages.

Coral's heart pounds as if there is a little woman inside it, bashing away on a toy drum the size of a thimble. It's not a monkey these days; it's a little woman, and she is furious. It's been pounding like that since Flint was born: it almost feels normal now. It's the real reason Coral can't sleep, she realises—not because she wants to stay awake and be productive. If this tablet helps, she is sure the little woman will be gone by morning.

Coral lies and waits, but the tablet doesn't work. She moves herself around on the bed, and pushes the bits of foam further into her ears, but she can hear Jasper talking to Flint; then, when they are silent, she can hear the fridge grumbling and her breath against the wool of the blanket. She feels as if she might never sleep again, and wonders if that could be possible.

After thrashing for what feels like hours, Coral decides to get up, because that's what you do when you can't sleep, isn't it, and she pulls on a dressing-gown and walks into the living room, where Jasper is asleep on the couch with the crib beside him.

When she stands over the crib and sees that Flint is sleeping too, a cool loneliness the colour of a blue sky sweeps through her body. It is a cool wind, the clouds, the shade on a spring afternoon, and it comes after a life of stuffiness and heat. Because of this, it is refreshing. Coral is so separate from everyone, right now, and always. She was born for a reason, but it wasn't to be a member of society, like Jasper is, like Flint will be. She realises now that she is here to help those who are really human, and she needs to get on with it. This is why she can't sleep: because she doesn't need to.

She gets to work. It is a good thing that Jasper is here—he can take care of Flint while Coral prepares, so that she can take care of all of them, properly, forever.

Her breasts are hurting, but the pain feels powerful, and it makes her insides shudder and shake, as if preparing for battle. She goes to the bathroom and pulls her pyjama pants down. There is no blood on the pad that is stuck to her undies—she is empty of what she needs to be. She does a wee, and stands and takes her singlet off. Her breasts are still big and foreign to her. They are red, and there is a rash on either end of one of them.

Coral places her cool palms against the hot breast skin and takes deep breaths into her diaphragm. It's important not to get overwhelmed now. She needs to be strong and keep busy.

⟡

Later, when Jasper wakes and Flint wakes and Coral is more awake than she ever has been in her entire life, Jasper takes one of her cracked hands in his, and stares at her. Before she can stand and move away, he asks her if they can try—again, properly, for the first time—to be together.

'For Flint,' he says, and then, 'because I love you.'

He can't possibly love her, and she laughs back at him before she can stop herself: laughs back at his big curled head and his strange kind of hope.

'Why are you laughing?' he asks.

Her reply is muffled by Flint's wriggling little body.

4

JASPER ISN'T HELPING, so Coral asks him to leave. She has been up for days, weeks, writing at the computer, cleaning up the pigsty around her in the breaks between inspiration. She is not hungry, she is not tired, and she knows what's going on. Jasper has been talking to Topaz and Ruby behind her back; Amber too, probably. They want to stop her from writing because they don't understand what she is doing.

The nurse keeps visiting, and one morning she asks Coral how she is feeling. Coral says she is feeling good, but the word comes out as if it means something different, and everything is upside down or turned sideways, and her tongue has stopped helping her mouth to say words. The nurse suggests that Coral do a test with her, 'just to see whether you might be a bit blue'. The nurse says this is common—'Lots of mums feel sad when their baby is little.' But Coral doesn't feel sad. She feels invincible.

After Coral answers the questions, the nurse's eyebrows furrow even more. 'So you haven't been feeling so sad or anxious that you can't sleep?'

Coral shakes her head. There's no need to talk about that.

'You're sleeping now?'

Yes, yes, yes, Coral nods.

'And you haven't had any thoughts of hurting yourself?'

Coral shakes her head again. The nurse doesn't want her to say that she has, or she would have asked more directly. Coral hasn't had thoughts of harming herself, anyway. She's telling the truth. She's got too much to do. She keeps shaking her head and smiling, with the whole of her face, the whole of her head, until the nurse leaves and they are alone again: her, the baby, and the blue stone. But not for long.

Topaz arrives. She is clicking her tongue so much that Coral has to ask her to stop.

'Let's get this place tidied up,' she says, and asks Coral where her garbage bags are kept.

'I don't know,' replies Coral, hoping this will suffice.

A pause, and then, 'You don't know, or you don't have any?'

Flint starts to cry, and Coral knows it's because of the angelite, and Topaz, and all the energies crashing against each other. She and her baby need a bit of time on their own, and no one wants to give it to them.

'Here,' her mother says, opening up her arms. 'Have a break, give him to me, sit on the couch, rest a little.'

There is no time for resting, no need for it. She will try to explain. 'No, Mum, it's okay. We're okay.'

Topaz stops her busying, and stands with her hands on her narrow hips. Her face has that look about it—the one that is disbelieving.

'I can work with Flint on my hip. It's better that way. And he needs a feed. Please, Mum.' Coral hears the beg in her voice and she forgives it.

'What on earth are you working on? It's not the time to be working on anything.'

The face in front of her—the one she has known the longest—warps, and then smooths out again, and Coral resists the urge to grab hold of the body below and shake it. Her thoughts start to chant: *The book won't write itself. The book won't write itself.* She knows this, but the reminder is useful. She must get back to work.

'I'm working on a book,' she says. 'And it won't write itself.'

Topaz makes a noise, and clicks her tongue, again and again. It hurts Coral's ears. She has never understood why Coral writes; her verbosity blinds her.

'Well. I can be with him while you write, if you must. Let me help.'

The woman comes towards her. Coral moves back to save the baby, and trips over an object on the kitchen floor. Before she falls, Flint is taken from her arms. She is lying on the lino, stomach against the cold. Her face is slack and oily.

Falling over makes Coral cry, and once she starts, she can't stop, until the taps turn off (like magic). She doesn't feel sad so much as bereft, of time and sleep and courage, but then she feels good again, and she wants her baby back. Topaz has put him in his cot, and is trying to tidy Coral's hair.

'Can we clean up properly tomorrow, Mum?' she asks, hoping for distance.

'Yes,' is the muted reply.

Coral is breathless; Coral has time, and she is grateful for it.

⟡

She sits holding Flint in her arms on the couch. It is morning, she is quite sure, and she can hear a few birds singing outside. She should find out what kind of birds they are. Why has she never wondered this before? she asks Flint, who is drifting between sleep and waking, his little face twisting and grimacing like an old man in pain. She knows he is not in pain, though—she is so bonded to him now. She has been told that babies make all sorts of funny and confusing faces, because they haven't yet learned how to make the right face for the right feeling, and so they smile when they are scared and grimace when they are contented. She rocks him gently, and wonders whether he needs a feed or a change or whether she can put him back in his cot and write another few paragraphs.

Her mobile rings: it's been doing that a lot, but she doesn't have the time to answer it. The noise of the ringtone makes Flint whimper, and then he appears to doze off again. Coral laughs, at his changeability, and what she has got herself in to. It doesn't feel scary now, but she knows it's a lot—having a child, being a mother, loving and teaching.

Flint opens his eyes again, then his pink mouth. He has no teeth. 'I am angry,' he says. 'I will kill you.'

Coral isn't surprised. She thought he might be murderous—after all, he is hers, and she has always been bloodthirsty. The way he says the words 'kill you' strikes Coral as funny: it is as if he might really do it, though she can't imagine how, when he is so small. Maybe she can talk him out of it.

'No, darling, you don't need to kill me. I have milk for you. I'll feed you again soon.'

She shushes him and clucks at him and says 'soon soon soon', over and over, until his eyes flutter and close. If she can just keep him sleeping, he won't do anything harmful. She will fill him up with milk again when he cries for it. He won't get hungry enough to kill her—she knows how to manage the urges, the anger of others.

There is a knock at the door, so she tiptoes with Flint to his crib and lays him down so gently that he could be a fairy in the woods sleeping on moss at the base of a big gnarled tree. He twists and grunts on his back, but his eyes stay closed. Coral tiptoes from the crib to the door, where the knocking has started up again. She wishes it would stop—it pounds like a headache.

Behind the door stands Amber.

'Coral, I've been trying to call,' she says, and she looks flustered, which is unusual for Amber but unsurprising, given all the banging.

Her hair is mussed at the top, and her breasts can be seen where her shirt has been pulled too far down on one side. Coral has never really seen Amber's breasts. They are divine, and it feels timely that they are more visible, on this day of eating and feeding and killing. A flash of her friend's breasts slashed and bloody enters Coral's mind, and then leaves. She winces at the red of it.

'I've been busy,' she tells Amber. There seems to be more answering-for after having a baby, more expectation that everyone will know what you are doing and where you are. Coral feels as if she is tightening against it, looking for where the escape hatch might be.

'Of course you have,' Amber answers, stone-faced. A smile wouldn't hurt, Coral reflects. 'Just answer your phone, though, okay?'

Promises not made are not promises, so Coral doesn't answer this, or nod her head, but merely lets Amber in, and sits on the couch with her. Flint is quiet in his crib, but Amber asks after him anyway, as if she needs to remind Coral that there is a baby to think about, as if Coral doesn't already know this in every part of her being. As if—and she won't tell Amber this, for it is none of Amber's business—Flint didn't just threaten to murder her, because he is angry, because she is.

She can't tell anyone that Flint is murderous, because he is more powerful than any of them realise and she has to make sure he doesn't lash out if he realises he is being cornered. She has given birth to a very important thing and only she can make sure he becomes what he has the potential to become, given time. She keeps her mouth shut about it, and answers Amber's questions easily, lightly, though Amber keeps frowning and picking up her phone to type things into it, as if she is taking notes.

Amber appears to be quizzing Coral too, which is unnecessary; she won't get to the bottom of anything.

'What did you have for lunch?'

'I haven't had any yet.'

'Yet?' Amber echoes. 'It's five o'clock in the afternoon!'

Coral knew this, she knew this—she could sense it without even needing to seek out the time. Amber needs someone to help her calm down. There's nothing to worry about.

'I ate a lot yesterday, don't worry, I'll eat soon, we will eat soon,' she says gently, like a lullaby. If she can put Amber to sleep, everything will be much easier to organise. From the other room, Flint starts to wail. He is trying to tell her that it's not the time for anyone to be sleeping, but she knows that babies don't know everything, even this one, and that lulling Amber into a doze will mean she can turn on the oven and prepare Flint for the dish without prying questions and hysteria.

Amber is staring at her now, not saying anything. Coral feels like she is being watched on a television.

'How did you sleep last night? Your mum told me you've got some sleeping tablets?'

She knew they were talking behind her back. Suggesting to each other that she isn't capable, and doesn't know any better, when she knows better than all of them. The anger is bile in her throat now. She likes the taste of it. This is why she hasn't been eating—she needs to be empty for the bile to rise.

'They don't work,' she says, despite herself.

'So you didn't sleep again?' Amber asks, face bunched like a paper bag.

'I slept a bit,' she says, though she didn't.

She hears a noise behind her—more whispers: who did Amber bring with her? who did she smuggle in?—but remains calm. They won't stop her from doing what she needs to do. If she can get Amber out of the house soon, it will be better.

'I think I'll try to sleep now,' she says, looking Amber square in the eye so there will be no way she can tell that Coral is lying.

She remembers that her breasts hurt, and cups them with both her hands. Amber raises her eyebrows—she has never liked displays of anything but decorum—but cupping her breasts helps them feel less vulnerable and so Coral keeps her hands where they are. They feel very warm in her palms—she should wash them, or something. Her face feels hot too, and her throat is tight and swollen.

'What's wrong?' Amber asks. 'Are you in pain?'

She won't tell Amber; she's not that slow. They will only try to control her, and she has a lot to do.

From the bedroom, she hears the angelite stone calling her. 'Coral? Coral. Coral!'

It has a voice like Flint's voice. Maybe she has been getting them confused.

'Hurry. Hurry,' it urges. 'You Don't Have Much Time.'

The light in the living room is so bright. Coral tries to remember if it has a dimmer. She can smell dirty nappies, though she is sure she threw them all out. She can smell her own milk, her own vagina. She feels sick, but in a way that will help keep her on track.

She shakes her head, so Amber won't ask her anything else.

'Then why are you holding yourself like that?'

She shakes her head again.

Amber is getting angry with her: she can tell by the shape of her mouth and her chin. 'Coral, speak to me!'

The pain in her breast stabs her inside, and she hears the

angelite's voice again. It is meaner; it growls this time. 'You Are All Alone. No One Loves You.'

Coral looks at Amber and sees that the creature from Poland is behind her, sprawled out on the floor in its dress, with that faraway look in its eye. The creature doesn't care about her. No one does.

She starts to cry. Amber holds her hand. She slowly tells Amber everything there is to worry about.

⟡

The team of people who come to look at her arrive quickly after Amber calls them, and calls Topaz, and Ruby, and later on Jasper, or so Coral assumes, because all of them end up there with her in her living room, hunched over like bats. Jasper gets Flint from the cot because he is crying, and he holds him well. Ruby holds him too: they all do. Coral doesn't warn them about the angelite when they go into the bedroom. She doesn't need to. The angelite won't bother with them; it only wants her.

All the people on the team are tall, and they speak softly and directly—looking at Coral's face in a way that seems like searching or listening. They ask her when she last slept, and she whispers, 'Never.' They ask her if there are voices in her head, but she won't tell them while the angelite is listening.

She feels scared. Topaz sits by her side, rubbing her arm and saying silly little things, when they ask her how her baby is. I don't know, she wants to say. Why don't you ask him?

When she kisses Flint goodbye, he opens his mouth and says, 'Fuck you.'

5

CORAL SPENDS THREE weeks in hospital on her own, and then she goes home and Topaz helps her with the baby. Her milk dries up during those weeks, but she doesn't care. She had mastitis, and because she left it so long the antibiotics need to be strong and taken for a while. They hurt her tummy and make her feel woozy, and it's a punishment she can endure.

She can't breastfeed Flint now. She doesn't tell anyone that she doesn't want to, anyway. Her breasts have deflated, and her milk wouldn't be good for him. It wouldn't feel right to hold him close.

They have told her to take a number of other tablets each day, and she has been since that first night in the hospital. She can't hear the angelite stone or her baby talking anymore. Maybe she misses them.

Time is flat, like a pancake. She feels nothing, and then she feels little things, like hunger, and then she feels big things, like anger, and horrendous, wet sadness. Sometimes when she looks at Flint she feels happy for a second, because he is so very charming. She wants him to love her again, if he ever did, but she doesn't know how to say sorry.

Topaz tells her he is bonny, and cheerful, and is sleeping like an angel on a cloud, feeding well from the bottle. This eases her guilt, but doesn't eliminate it.

Flashes of the hospital come to her when she is alone, which is not often, with everyone flickering around her house like moths. She was scared there—it was so bright, and the lights hurt her eyes, and they wouldn't turn them all off even in the dead of the night. She knows she said weird things and had strange ideas—the ideas are still there just at the back of her brain—but she doesn't feel ashamed. She knows that it was psychosis, and that she was vulnerable to it, because she has been sick since she was little.

They didn't tell her it was psychosis, not directly, as if they were ashamed on her behalf. The psychiatrist at the hospital was a stooped, balding man with a tendency to clear his throat more often than surely was necessary, and he could hardly look at her. He was kind, though, in his nervous way. He told her she'd had a rough time of it, and that her baby would be so happy to have her home again.

✧

The tablets start to move the strange thoughts from the back of her brain out of her head entirely, and a woman who calls herself a parent–infant therapist comes twice a week to sit with

Coral and Flint and help them get to know each other. Something stirs in Coral's chest sometimes when she looks at Flint, and she tries not to let it overwhelm her. He doesn't open his mouth and speak anymore, and he seems quite contented. His face moves about, making smirk after smile after grimace. This is how babies learn, though it also might be gas, the woman tells her. When the gas makes him smile, Coral is told to pretend that he is really smiling.

She holds him close to her chest a lot: skin to skin. He purrs, her little kitten. The therapist suggests that Coral's instincts are best, and encourages her to be the mum she wants to be, dreams of being.

Ruby comes for tea, and they eat takeaway curry laksa and pass Flint between them. Coral feels tears come to her eyes as they swoon over how beautiful he is—she seems to be on the verge of crying most of the time now, and it's not so bad. She is sleeping and she is eating, and it has to come out somehow. Flint drinks up all the expensive formula she gives him, as if it is just what he needs.

There is pressure to try feeding him with her breasts again. She floats above it, wondering how she would feel about the pressure if she wasn't so full of medication, knowing she would be upset and angry and anxious, that she would be trying to swat away the shame. She doesn't react, just smiles at what they say, her body a loose harness on her back, letting her roam. She remembers what one kind nurse said when she was in the hospital, crying about never breastfeeding her baby again: 'Fed is best, not breastfed is best. *Fed* is best.'

⟡

As the weeks pass, sometimes Coral wonders why this happened to her. Not just the postnatal psychotic break and the hospital admission, but the OCD, and the pregnancy, and the motherhood. She concludes nothing, because there is nothing to understand. Life is unfair and life is fateful. Coral has never made the rules. She doesn't know if she will do it well—the mothering, the caregiving, the parenting. She does know for certain, now, that Flint was sent from somewhere.

They get to know each other, finally, as he grows. He is a bold little boy—fearless and strong in a way that isn't familiar to Coral until it is, and she sees him as hers, her as his. He was born on the first of October and so he is a Libra, an air sign. Coral can tell by the way he breathes that he is meant to be here. He seems to love her (grabs for her with his chubby hands, rests his silky head on her body as if it is a comfort), and she understands deep inside that she loves him. It doesn't feel like the love she has for others: for Topaz, for Amber and Ruby, for her late grandmother. It fills her up and seeps from her pores; it changes the shape of her.

Flint laughs, and sometimes he cries, but she is told by other mothers that he is calm, and brave, and that he doesn't fuss as much as their children do. Coral wonders what this means, but with motherhood comes some acceptance, and she doesn't ponder too long.

⟡

One morning at the park, she and Flint go down the slide together and she plays with him in the tanbark next to the sandpit because he prefers the texture. When she reaches out her arms to pick him up he reaches back and says something like *mama*, even though he is too young to say a proper word and it is likely just a serendipitous sound. It delights her, and she snuffles her nose and cheeks against his to feel his softness. Thereafter—after Flint has announced her—she feels mothering in the pit of her stomach: an orb. She can't mould it and she can't touch it, but it is there.

No one else seems able to make him laugh the way she can. She stores this in her mother orb. She lets others love him and hold him. She is occasionally serene. It is hard too—dreadfully hard. She weeps, she is so tired, and she feels lonely. Flint isn't everything: he can't be. She sighs her way through the silences, and cries through the sound of his screams.

⟡

In April, when Flint is six months old, Topaz asks if she can throw him a little party, which is ridiculous but heart-warming, and just what they all need. There is fairy bread, and Topaz and her friends set up Coral's tiny courtyard to look like a rainbow. Topaz is different these days, or Coral is, or they both are. Coral sees loyalty shining through her mother's eyes, though she can still be magnificently tiresome.

Ruby, and Amber and Micah, and Jasper come to the party: they seem delighted to celebrate her baby. Coral is rested, Flint is rested, and he sucks on a rusk stick and falls asleep in her arms.

'I'm sorry about that stone I gave you,' Ruby says quietly, as they stand together enjoying the scene, under the birch tree that fills the courtyard.

Coral has to ask her what she means.

'The angelite stone. It made you sick.'

Coral laughs before she can stop herself, then looks at Ruby, into her eyes, and grabs her warm fingers. 'Ruby! No. It wasn't the stone.'

What it was, she doesn't know. But it wasn't the stone.

The day is mild and blue, and the party goes for hours.

Coral sees the creature from Poland in the mirror behind her when she goes to the bathroom, brighter and softer than it used to be. It comes to visit infrequently now, and only when she can bear it. The creature is there to remind Coral that this story is hers.

Acknowledgments

I live and write in Narrm, and I need to acknowledge and thank the traditional custodians of this land, the Wurundjeri People. I also need to thank the Awabakal and Worimi People, the traditional custodians of Muloobinba, where I wrote a large section of this book.

Thank you to my editor, David Winter, who knew what *Plum* could be, and helped me get her there. To the whole team at Text: thank you for supporting my writing so wholeheartedly, and with such skill and care.

Thank you to the Book 2 Alliance, and to my early readers: Ronnie, Ellena, Otto. And to the writers who generously read *Plum*—Ronnie Scott, Ellena Savage, Hannah Kent, Stephanie Bishop, and Amanda Lohrey. I'm so grateful. To my studio gang at the Nicholas Building and to the space itself: thank you; thank goodness for you. I also need to thank my Polish friends, Anna Manarczyk and Emilia Bachem, for your help when I needed specific Polish details, and for being the reason I have been lucky enough to visit Poland twice. I would also like to pay my respects to the late Polish artist Emilia Bartkowska, whose beautiful, haunted artworks appear in *Plum*, and whose creature will always be with us.

My friends, the ones who don't write and the ones who do—thank you for standing by and for reminding me there is more to life than reading and writing. You make me laugh and make me happy. My family—thank you for loving me, trying to keep me grounded, and for never not having a book in your hands. To my husband, Otto—I couldn't have written *Plum* without your unfailing support. You're wonderful.

To my therapist, my sponsor, and my twelve-step family—thank you for taking care of me, and for letting me stand on my own two feet when I can. I am sick without my support network, like every other human being.

To the women I worked with at PANDA from 2016 to 2021: this book is for you. I learnt everything I know and everything I don't know from the time I spent with you all—such wise, congruent, compassionate leaders, and the most beautiful friends I could have imagined.

Finally, to the parents who suffer through the hardest of all the jobs—thank you. A special thanks with deep gratitude to those parents who trusted me with their stories, their fears, and their private realities during my time as a counsellor and supervisor at PANDA. Your children are so lucky to have you!

To all parents in the perinatal period, with your bleary heads and your raw hearts: I hope you can remind yourselves that you are only human; that you are worthy and deserving because you exist; that you have the expert within you.